T0328866

graffiti girl

graffiti girl
kelly parra

POCKET BOOKS   MTV BOOKS
New York   London   Toronto   Sydney

POCKET BOOKS, a division of Simon & Schuster, Inc.
1230 Avenue of the Americas, New York, NY 10020

Library of Congress Cataloging-in-Publication Data

Parra, Kelly.
  Graffiti girl / by Kelly Parra.
    p. cm.
  Summary: A Mexican American high school student in a small California town is drawn into the underground world of graffiti art, feeling that it is the only way to express herself artistically and still remain true to her cultural identity.
    ISBN-13: 978-1-4165-3461-7
    ISBN-10:   1-4165-3461-X
  [1. Graffiti—Fiction. 2. Mexican Americans—Fiction. 3. Self-acceptance—Fiction. 4. High schools—Fiction. 5. Schools—Fiction. 6. Interpersonal relations—Fiction. 7. California—Fiction.] I. Title.
  PZ7.P2448Gr 2007
  [Fic]—dc22

                                                                        2006036967

This MTV Books/Pocket Books trade paperback edition May 2007

10 9 8 7 6 5 4 3 2 1

Manufactured in the United States of America

For information regarding special discounts for bulk purchases, please contact Simon & Schuster Special Sales at 1-800-456-6798 or business@simonandschuster.com.

For Ethan, because you knew me in my teen days and have shared first experiences with me ever since. I love you forever.

Acknowledgments

Many thanks to the talented Tina Ferraro, who has been with me every step of the way with this novel. Dianna Love Snell, a gifted writer and artist always willing to lend a helping hand no matter where she is in the world. Kristin Nelson, savvy and awesome, for believing in my writing and helping to make this story come alive. Jennifer Heddle and Lauren McKenna for seeing something in *Graffiti Girl* and giving her a home, and Carly Sommerstein, Erica Feldon, and Lisa Litwack for their wonderful work. I can't forget the Monterey

Bay Chapter for all the support through the years. The online graffiti experts who helped bring me into the graf lifestyle, any errors are all my own. Esther Moss, one of the strongest women I know, thank you for teaching me to be the same. Evan and Samantha, with this book I hope I taught you that you can be anything you want to be as long as you believe.

A shout out to the folks at MTV and to all the artists out there, who make our world a little more beautiful with each masterpiece you create. You rock.

chapter one

GRAFFITI BACKGROUND
The Design Painted Behind a Piece
to Make It Look Awesome
       –Angel's Piecebook Notes
       (A little about my background.)

"Three bucks for a typical doctor's note. Want me to get creative, the price is five."

"Five's a rip-off."

I lifted my shoulder, taking a quick scan of the hallway for lurking school officials. But I wasn't really into the sale. "Your choice. I'm not the one who's afraid of Daddy finding out I ditched."

Selena Macgregor, a North Homestead High junior prep,

hugged her purple binder to her chest, pinning me with a look that had "bitch" written all over it.

Her pastel pink lip curled. "At least I have a daddy."

My mouth curved. The *chica* would have to do better than bash the man I had never met to get under my skin. "You say that as if it's a good thing."

Leaning against my locker, I slipped my hand into the pocket of my faded army cargo pants and felt for the thirteen bucks I'd already made that morning. I had the rep of looking at someone's handwriting and forging the style. But dealing with chicks who acted like they were better than everyone else sometimes made that talent my worst enemy.

A guy from my English lit class cruised by. "What's up, Angel?"

"Hey, Ramón." I nodded, checking out the other kids filing into the hallway coming from lunch.

That slow tightening in my stomach began.

Almost time.

"Beth, how much longer till fifth?" Didn't want to be late for the only class I gave a damn about. Especially today.

No answer from Beth.

Six lockers to my left, my best friend's thick, curvy body was pressed close to a sophomore's lanky one. A guy she'd gone out with a couple of times. When I said "gone out," I wasn't talking dates, but the tongue-down-the-throat hook-up.

Beth's blonde curls brushed her shoulders as she talked flirtatiously with—damn, forgot his name—the sophomore kid.

"Tough to get Bethany Malone's attention when she's in slut mode."

My expression went hard. I met Selena's gaze. "Take a walk."

Her eyes widened. "What about my dismissal note?"

"Gee, shop's suddenly closed."

"Bitch," she hissed, turning away.

"Skank."

I pivoted, shaking off the tension wedged between my shoulders. Spun the combo to my locker and lifted the metal tab. Shoving a stack of blank excuse slips to the back of the small metal space, I pulled out my black pack. Two Sharpie pens and a charcoal pencil rolled forward. I caught them before they slid off the edge, then slammed the door shut.

Leaning down to hook my fingers through the handle of my portfolio case, my heavy, wavy ponytail fell over my shoulder. I flipped it back. My unmanageable hair irritated me to no end. More than once, I wished I could grab the nearest pair of scissors and hack it all off. But anybody who had to deal with a mass of thick hair knew that if you chopped it, it looked like one big hair puff surrounding your head. Learned that hard truth in third grade.

"Come on, Beth. We have to roll."

" 'Bye," Beth said to the sophomore and strolled over to me. Her full cheeks were pink, her blue eyes laughing. "Brian's kinda cute."

Brian, right.

Needless to say, Beth really liked guys.

"Yeah," I said. "Great."

Usually I'd joke about Beth making out with a lower classman since we had junior status, but today my thoughts zeroed in a different direction.

Beth pulled out a wrapped hard candy the color of a strawberry from her pocket, twisted off the plastic wrap, and stuck it her mouth. "Selena Macgregor pay for a note?"

"Nah, I passed. She got on my nerves."

Beth winced. "She's so stuck-up."

"Tell me about it. I'll catch you in economics."

"Yep. Good luck with the presentation."

I tightened my grip on the plastic handle. "Thanks." Truth was, I needed all the luck I could manage.

Jogging past posters taped on pale Pepto-Bismo–colored walls advertising cheesy North Homestead High events, I slipped into the art room just as the bell rang. I smelled the familiar nose-wrinkling disinfectant. At the end of each class, the students had to clean up their current project mess with the pale blue spray bottles under the sink. Sometimes people went overboard. I glanced at the other kids in the class, either sitting or moving around the room. My competition. The long art tables and the storage cabinets were usually a comforting sight, acknowledging that I was in a place of creative freedom. But now the place only reminded me that today I'd discover if my dream could ever become a reality.

Mierda, my mouth was actually dry.

I set my case on the art table, blew a wayward tendril of hair out of my face, and hooked my pack on the back of a wooden chair. When I sat down, the old screws in the chair squeaked. I glanced at Mr. Chun. He was setting up a wooden easel in front of the class. I slid a finger across the soft surface of my bottom lip. Smooth, until I hit the corner and found a rough spot. Adding my thumb, I tugged at the dead skin. Yeah, a nervous habit.

"I'll show you mine, if you show me yours."

I jerked my fingers away, taking a tiny lip peeling with me. Rubbing it off against my thigh, I shifted my attention to the art table aligning mine. Nathan Ramos—NHH's senior track star, and an amazing artist—sat across from me. His hazel eyes glanced at my portfolio case.

"Not a chance, Jack." During two years of art classes and the wonders of alphabetized seating, we'd learned to joke around with each another and become friends.

Never more than that.

I definitely wasn't one of those glam girls I'd seen him with around school, who sported halter tops, gobs of makeup, and a matching purse. He was a popular jock, after all, and like a magnet sucked all the preppy snobs to him on a regular basis. Not to mention, my beige skin and dark hair had no similarity to his light-skinned, blonde—on again, off again—girlfriend, Misty Peterson. Maybe it was the kick-back, frayed jeans I usually sported, or the tees with cartoon characters. Whatever reason, I somehow managed to attract guy "pals" like magnets.

Nathan being my hands-down best catch.

My lips twitched. "Wouldn't want to put your presentation to shame, anyway."

A slow smile curved his mouth. "Yeah, that would pretty much suck."

We both knew what I said was a load of bullshit.

I wasn't lying when I referred to Nathan as an amazing artist. His work was "exquisite," as Mr. Chun liked to put it. Nathan studied an arranged bowl of fruit, transferred it on to canvas with such awesome use of line, shading, and depth, it felt as if you could reach out and pluck a pear from the painting.

Me? I freaking wish.

The only thing I could bring to life on paper or canvas was a carrot for Bugs Bunny. But the day I'd admit my insecurities to anyone would be the day Brangelina stopped making headlines.

Nathan leaned casually back in his seat, turning an art gum eraser between his thumb and finger and letting it hit the table once, twice. A white cotton T-shirt stretched across his toned shoulders and chest. Overgrown brown hair with mahogany highlights fell in a finger-combed disarray. A Lance Armstrong yellow band wrapped around his tan wrist.

His carefree style was . . . seriously hot.

"Come on, Angel, I'm up for some comp. Let me have a quick look."

I ignored the butterflies in my stomach. "You'll have to wait with the rest of class and be awed all at once."

He let out that nice laugh.

Great laugh. Great confidence.

The guy was one big Great at everything he did. Probably why I tried not to crush on him too much. We were as opposite as night was to day, and I wasn't just talking about our art. From what I knew, Nathan was second-generation Mexican-American. I was third-generation, and, not to mention, half-white. Nathan was a cool guy, but even though he wore casual clothes, there was something about his personality, his cool style that clued you in he came from money and was likely going places.

I didn't. I wasn't. Enough said.

Nathan also stood a good chance of landing top honors with his presentation. Advanced art was comprised of twenty upperclassmen who'd already taken two consecutive years of art electives. We weren't all great artists, but deep inside we strived to be. That was the way it was for me, anyway. And we were all competing to get the lead position on the mural committee to paint the new Viking mascot scene in the school's courtyard by drawing a mock mural design—also a required project grade for our class.

A position I wanted so badly I could practically taste it.

Something I'd never be caught dead admitting out loud. I wasn't known for being a NHH advocate. But there was a lot more to this deal than some school mural project. The three high schools in town were going through the same selection process to decide who would design their courtyard mural and compete in an overall community endeavor to paint the town's cultural history on public park walls and selected historical sites. There was even some kind of scholarship award attached, but that wasn't why I wanted to be a part of this so much.

"Showtime," Nathan murmured, nodding to the head of the class.

"Okay," Mr. Chun called out, interrupting the murmurs of random voices. "Let's get the presentations started." He scanned a sheet on his desk, and then called out, "Miguel Badalin?"

No one said a word.

Miguel Badalin, all around Latino badass, wasn't in attendance. Yet.

Like that was a big surprise.

He had a rep for being tardy and ditching class when he felt like it. Never bothered to cross my path for a forged note, either. I didn't know how he skated through school. But in the past, we'd ended up in the same after-school detention more times than I could count.

Miguel couldn't be competition, anyway, because of his attendance record. There was criteria that had to be met to head the mural committee. Stuff like good attendance and a 3.0 grade average. I was barely meeting the terms myself.

Yeah, Badalin was like *Fear Factor*: "Evidently attending class isn't a factor for you."

The door swung open and in walked Miguel.

Shocker.

He wore baggy jeans that fit low on his narrow hips, a silver wallet chain slapping his thigh as he walked. A loose, long-sleeve thermal top with *"Independiente"* printed across his chest. Black hair buzzed close to the sides of his head, yet spiky on top. And he carried a portfolio case, too. One of his partners-in-crime followed behind. Didn't remember his name, but Miguel always had someone with him at all times.

"Ah, Mr. Badalin, just in time for your presentation."

"Eh, glad to hear it. Here's my excuse slip."

So this time he was covered.

Sure my head had been in an art cloud this past month working my butt off on my presentation, but maybe the guy had been coming to class on time these past few weeks. Not that I cared one way or the other.

Mr. Chun raised his stubby, faint brows and took the note. "Thank you. We are ready when you are. When your friend joins his own class."

A few students let out a laugh as Miguel's friend took off.

I glanced at Nathan, but he wasn't looking at me. He was aiming a long stare in Miguel's direction. A stare Miguel returned. Not the first time I'd seen the same intense look pass between them, but I'd never gotten the nerve to ask why. Not my business.

Didn't stop the niggling curiosity, though.

The friction between the two couldn't be that Nathan thought Miguel was any artistic competition for him. Miguel and I leaned toward the same use of bright color and strong lines, a total 180 from Nathan's skill. Miguel's style was almost abstract, which added clout to the rumors that Miguel practiced graffiti art. That he was a "tagger," and roamed the dark streets of Homestead with his "Brown Pride" posse and a backpack full of spray paint.

But I'd seen so many reps ruined by false rumors, I made it a policy not to believe everything I heard unless seen by my own dark eyes.

Miguel cruised to the front of the class to the easel display turned away from everyone, set his display board up, and then swiveled it around. He leaned his weight on his right foot and tilted his head to the side as he waited—a total couldn't-give-a-F attitude.

The class was as quiet as a tomb.

Style.

This was the one word that first came to me. Miguel presented a Viking scene so exceptional, everyone had to be amazed. The intense colors and jagged points were his trademark, but the Viking, the ship, and the North Homestead Vikings title—same aspects each student had to produce in their design—were clean and detailed. The design had flare. Dark smooth lines outlined each aspect. Bold, contrasting colors grabbed your attention. It was modern. Hip. I could totally see this as a mural design.

Mierda, more talent to beat.

"Miguel, this is by far your best work!" Mr. Chun walked over and patted Miguel on his shoulder. The guy didn't seem to mind as he slid a glance first to Nathan, and then to me.

And smiled.

Not one of those hey-buddy grins I usually got, either, but an almost flirtatious one.

The smile was so unexpected I curved my lips back at him, then flicked my gaze down at the table, focusing on the old scratches embedded in the wood.

Nathan cleared his throat.

I shifted in my seat and looked at him.

He studied me, eyes narrowed in concentration, mouth in a straight line.

"What?" I asked, brushing a strand of hair out of my vision.

He lifted a shoulder and looked away.

What the hell did I do?

The clock ticked closer to the bell with three more presentations left—Nathan's, Lydia Wesley's, and mine in between them.

I rubbed my thumb against the plastic handle of my art case.

Nathan set up his board, while Miguel pulled up a chair and . . . sat at my table. I remained still, acting like I didn't care, even though I could totally see what he was doing in my peripheral vision. Mr. Chun was a pretty laid-back teacher, let us work where we wanted, go on errands during class, as long as we did our work and didn't abuse his trust. But, hell yeah, I was surprised to have Miguel Badalin come sit by me since we hadn't exactly participated in a conversation that involved more than a "what's up?" before.

"Eh, how's it goin'?"

I looked to my right. He glanced at me, then looked toward the head of the class. I had to admit he had a really nice smile. Even with the one crooked incisor tooth. "All right."

"You look a little nervous."

Terrific, was it stamped on my forehead? I lifted a shoulder.

"What for?" His good-looking face scrunched up a moment, then smoothed out as he slouched comfortably in his chair, legs spread, arms crossed. "Just a class project. No big deal."

Right. "If it's not a big deal, what about yours? Your presentation was good. Like you put more effort in than usual." I waited for him to get offended, or get up and sit somewhere else. You just never knew how an artist would take a comment like that. Artwork was sacred to the artist. We hated to know when our work was crap and loved when people praised it. I'd given a twisted compliment.

But he just said, "Yeah, looks like it wasn't enough," and his eyes were on Nathan.

Nathan had turned his easel, revealing his board to the class, and then stuffed his hands in the front pockets of his faded blue jeans. Like his other creations, this one was awesome.

Real, perfect, just like the guy himself.

The Viking stood masculine and rough, as if he could step right off the ship and into our classroom. The shading was delicate, giving light where there was only board, and darkness that had depth. I could tell he used acrylics and watercolor, maybe even oil pastels—blending media was something I experimented with—to give a soft blend to the clouds and the sun that peered down on the swaying ocean. The school name didn't look out of place even though it floated in the sky in curvy block letters.

I stared with awe and even envy. To create such realism and beauty was a dream of mine. I looked down at my portfolio case.

Yeah, I was glad for Nathan, to have the class "ooh" and "aah," and for Mr. Chun to beam and actually clap in recognition of such kick-ass detail, but I felt my stomach slowly tighten into a serious knot. For the first time I wasn't too thrilled to have Nathan's last name close to mine.

Because now my presentation had to follow the best in the class.

"Angel Rodriguez?"

I forced my gaze in Mr. Chun's direction.

He lifted those stubby brows. "You're up."

Great.

chapter two

DRIPS
Spray Paint Application That Runs with Streaks;
A Mark of an Artist Who Sucks Big Time
> —Angel's Piecebook Notes
> *(Sometimes I suck big time.)*

I wrapped a death grip around the handle of my portfolio case and rose from my seat. The plastic still slid within my sweaty grip.

"Good luck," Miguel said to me.

Was it my imagination or did his eyes add, *You're going to need it?* I muttered "thanks" and cruised to where I didn't want to go, the head of the class.

Nathan gave his project board to Mr. Chun. When he

walked by me, he smiled and whispered, "I'm ready to be awed."

Should have kept my big mouth shut.

The ancient wooden easel was already turned away from the class, so I set my portfolio on the small table beside it. My gaze moved across the room. No one was paying attention. Some kids where sketching, others chatting. Something I wasn't totally against since being the center of attention always made my heart speed up. But still, the possibility of them thinking the winner was pretty much in the bag with Nathan's dazzle-me design totally sucked.

Brushing hair out of my face, I took a breath that came out shaky. *Keep it cool, Rodriguez.* I unzipped my case, hesitantly raised the flap, and stared at my work.

My Viking was as realistic as I could draw him, but I had to be honest with myself. The *hombre* looked two-dimensional instead of three. The ocean waves were jagged, instead of soft and flowing. My use of rich colors and thick lines definitely drew the eye. But where was the realism? Where was the use of delicate shading that brought art to life?

It wasn't there, no matter how hard I tried. I knew it was my style, but more than once I wished I had a lighter hand. Even though I had worked my butt off on this presentation, sketched it out three times before settling on a design, and then painstakingly obsessed over color and medium, I had the same irritating thought in the back of my head.

Just not perfect.

"Angel?"

I looked at Mr. Chun.

"We're waiting."

"Right." My back tight and unyielding, I picked up the lightweight fifteen-by-fifteen-inch project board and set it on the easel, then slowly turned it toward the class. I felt like a robot—all stiff and forcing myself to do something I didn't want to do. Shifting my stance, I kicked the sole of my right K-Swiss against the floor once and stuffed my hands in the front pocket of my pullover sweatshirt.

Silence filled the room for what had to be the three most grueling seconds of my entire life. Just kill me now.

Finally someone said, "Nice color."

"Yeah," someone else agreed.

I licked my lips.

"Come on," Mike Grayson added, a total jerk who was always on somebody's case. "Since when have you seen a dark-skinned Viking sportin' a goatee? And Mexican hats and blankets for cargo? Get real."

I slid Grayson a look. "Can't get any more real than this."

"The fact that she added Latino symbolism is cool," Nathan said. "Makes her design unique because it shows a part of who she is."

"Blew her chances, all I gotta say."

Inside the pocket of my sweatshirt, my hand clenched into a fist.

"That's enough, Mike," Mr. Chun cut in. "Very eye-catching design, Angel. I enjoy your use of flow, and your style . . ."

I let out a soft breath and glanced at Nathan, who winked in return. Maybe I *had* pulled off a winning design. Then Nathan's expression went sort of blank as he looked over at Miguel, who said something to him.

I returned my attention to Mr. Chun.

". . . it's very whimsical," he finished with a smile.

And my pleasure vanished like that.

Whimsical, as in cartoony, as in not realistic.

As in not good enough.

Never good enough.

Someone coughed. Warmth heated my face and I willed myself to move.

The next moments went by in a blur. I turned in my project and went to my seat until the last presentation was given. Miguel had returned to his own table and I didn't feel up to any teasing with Nathan. So I completely ignored him during the rest of the class.

When the bell sounded, I grabbed my pack, sprang to my feet, and beelined out the door.

A firm hand landed on my shoulder halfway down the hallway. I jerked it off and turned around. So sue me, I wasn't in the best mood.

Nathan. His eyes searched mine. "What's the rush, Angel?"

I stepped to the right out of the stream of passing students, letting my gaze travel the hallway. As if I were actually seeing them. Hah. I could only see Mr. Chun calling my work "whimsical." Freaking *whimsical.* Damn it. "Just trying to get to class on time."

This was sort of a lie. Yeah, I was going to my next class, but I would have loved to ditch right now. Decompress. Vent some serious frustration. Problem was I'd ditched two days ago, already forged a note this week. The Office Brigade got suspicious with too many missed classes. A pattern, they liked to call it. And if by some slim chance I won the mural contest—I know, not going to happen—I'd hate myself if I messed up my chances.

"Don't talk about it, then."

I looked at him. His expression went distant as if I'd really had his attention, then lost it. "There's nothing—"

"You forgot something." He held his binder propped against his right hip and two portfolio cases in the other.

Right, the one thing I hadn't let out of my sight for the past three weeks and I forget about it just like that. *Smooth one, Rodriguez.* But since it was empty now I guessed it didn't really matter. I took the case, my fingers brushing his. "Thanks."

"Not a problem. Look, don't listen to Grayson. He's an idiot. Your design was created from something inside you. I know the feeling."

There he went being the nice guy again. And here I went being ignorant because I hadn't even told him how great his turned out. I nodded my head toward him. "Yours was great, too. I know you'll be a finalist."

Mr. Chun would show his favorites to the school faculty members for discussion and announce the winner during class on Monday. Three days of waiting . . .

For a clarification of defeat? For another letdown?

Probably.

Nathan finally smiled again, showing straight white teeth—a grin that always made me feel like he really enjoyed joking with me. Like we were really friends. "Stop, Angel. You're flattering me."

My lips curved in return. But my smile fell flat when Misty Peterson—Nathan's on-again, off-again girlfriend—strolled over, a book hugged against her "perky" chest, and bumped his portfolio case with her hip.

"Ready for a run?" she asked him in that confident yet feminine tone. Her long lashes were dark and curved, skin flawless. Lips covered in a light gloss and hair long and styled without a wayward strand in sight. How did she even manage that? For some reason strands of my hair were constantly falling out of my head and thick baby hairs sprang out of the top of my scalp all the time. Annoyed the hell out of me.

"Yeah, sure."

She looked at me. "Hi. Angel, right?"

"How's it goin'?" I think we were introduced once, but she still remembered my name. The thing was, no matter how much I would have not wanted to have liked Misty Peterson just for being Nathan's pretty girlfriend, I couldn't. I called people like I saw them, and Misty was an all right *chica.*

A rare form in high school, and a perfect match for Nathan.

"See you later," Nathan said, and they both turned and walked away to have that run.

Whatever.

"Mr. Torres kind of makes economics fun," Beth said to me after our last class as I picked the books out of my locker I needed for homework, which was disgustingly almost all of them.

"I guess."

"Like how he throws candy bars to us when we answer a question right. Not that I need any more candy bars."

I glanced at her. "Beth, you look great."

"Yeah, right. *You* look great."

I just rolled a shoulder. Beth had this thing about complimenting me, but I knew I wasn't anything special. Just another Mexican-American, like many of the other North Homestead High females of Latino descent in Homestead's small agricultural community. I figured I pretty much blended within the crowd.

Beth was what you'd call a voluptuous girl. Not fat with pounds, but kind of big boned. She sported a lot more curves than me, especially in the front. But for some reason, Beth didn't know how pretty she was with her dark blue eyes and killer long lashes. You'd think with all the guys she hooked up with, she'd get a clue. Some guys were jerks, hooked up with anyone who'd have them and didn't bother looking back, but she had to know they wouldn't keep coming around her if she was dog ugly, right?

It might seem weird that Beth and I were even friends since we were so different on the outside, with her light complexion and my darker, but other kids sometimes forgot that I wasn't full-blooded Mexican. I had friends who were, and spoke Spanish to one another in hallways, but I didn't hang with them. Besides, I'd known for a long time friendships were formed from within a person, not the color of their skin. The ones that mattered, anyway.

Beth and I had a fairly new best friend relationship. We'd only started hanging out our freshman year, when we'd landed in world affairs class together and had been paired up on a presentation. Beth had done most of the research—school stuff just came easier to her—and I'd managed the visual presentation. Pretty soon we were laughing at each other's jokes and making fun of all the preppy girls around school who always snubbed their noses at our kick-back clothes of faded jeans and tees. Then gradually we started hanging out and going to parties together. Last year, we'd become pretty much inseparable.

"Oh God," Beth said. "You are not going to believe who's got his eyes on you, walking this way." Beth was also easily excitable and it always came out through her expressive face. Right now her eyebrows were raised, her mouth slightly opened, and a hand floated midway in the air as if she needed to cover her mouth.

"Who? Nathan?"

"Eh, Angel," said a laid-back voice.

I turned to who sounded suspiciously like Miguel Badalin.

And . . . I wasn't so disappointed that it wasn't Nathan.

"Hey." Yeah, it was Miguel, with a different friend at his side. This guy's name I knew, Derek Mendoza. A junior, too, he had been in my last year's English class. I felt Beth nudge me with her binder. "This is my friend, Beth. Beth, Miguel and Derek."

"Hi," Beth said in that bright voice she reserved for guys.

I mentally rolled my eyes.

Derek said, "What's up?"

Miguel focused on me. He had this way of looking at you with a half smile that gave the impression he had a secret and wasn't going to tell. Somehow it intrigued me. "Wanted to know if you guys want to come hang out at my house right now. A few of us chill there till the *padre* gets home."

"Why?" popped out of my mouth before I could stop it. I was just a little shocked by the sudden invite.

"Damn, whatya think?" Derek blurted. "To kick back."

I offered Derek a bored look. "Maybe I don't want to kick it with you."

"Chill, Derek. I live a couple a blocks from here," Miguel

added. "Thought you might want to check out some of my pieces."

When Miguel said "pieces," he spoke my language. Art. But still, I hardly knew the guy.

"Your art's cool. I think I've got some stuff you might like."

So he thought my stuff was cool. Interesting. "Like what?"

"Come find out."

I looked at Beth and she smiled, giving me the *let's do this* sign with her eyes. Why not? It's not like it mattered what time I got home since my mom had the late shift at the restaurant. I should try to make it home by dinner so Nana didn't have to eat alone, though.

"All right," I finally agreed.

He nodded toward the exit, slipping on tinted black wraparound sunglasses. "Cool. This way."

The last of the students slowly emptied the hallway and we followed Miguel and Derek out toward the school parking lot. I tried not to laugh at Derek because he kind of walked like a duck—toes out and waddling. Derek was a guy who wore everything two sizes too big. I didn't know if it was because he was a stout, big guy or what, but his pants sagged, bunching at his ankles. And his shoes were usually untied with the tongue sticking up for the entire world to see. Ignorant.

The day was muggy with sporadic gray clouds dotting the sky. The afternoon wind carried the odor of cow crap. No joke. Homestead was an agricultural community with fields of vegetation such as strawberries, lettuce, and broc-coli, all surrounding the town's homes and building devel-opments, which was the primary reason our town was heavily Latino-oriented. Mexican families, like my grand-parents, had moved here to work in the fields and raise their families. Many of the families were on the north side of town, where I lived. Homestead, California, was actually about twenty minutes from the beach, and more often than not the ocean wind rolled in from the Pacific during late af-ternoon. So on the days the sun was harsh, the heat baked the fields and the wind helped give the community a nice whiff of fertilizer. Living here my whole life, I'd never gotten used to the smell.

"Damn, it stinks," Derek hissed.

Apparently, I wasn't the only one.

When Miguel led us into the parking lot, I said, "We're not walking?"

Derek laughed. "Miguel is a senior, dawg. Seniors don't walk."

Miguel didn't comment. I guess Derek spoke for both of them.

We strolled to an older model two-door black Blazer. The ride was cool, with tinted windows and the way it was low-ered almost to the ground. The tires had these shiny chrome rims that I'd seen a lot on *Pimp My Ride*.

"Nice wheels," Beth said.

"Suits me," Miguel said, and clicked a small key ring that

made a *beep* sound come from his Blazer. Probably housed a good stereo system, too.

He opened the door, took my portfolio case, and set it inside. What was up with the gentleman routine? He so didn't look the type.

Miguel's head slowly tilted down, then up as if he was measuring me. It made me hesitate.

When it came to guys, no dust settled on Beth. She was already stepping into the backseat.

I hooked my thumbs into the shoulder straps of my pack.

"What's up?" Miguel wanted to know, his lips curving. "Change your mind?" His tone was just shy of smartass.

"Did I say I changed my mind?"

I couldn't see his eyes, but when he didn't respond I figured he was surprised I'd talk attitude to him. I'm sure he was used to getting his ass kissed by the guys who followed him around as if he were some kind of god. No way did I consider him like that, cool senior artist or not. I just didn't get his sudden interest in me. He was Miguel Badalin—a senior whose name was said with awe because he had a rep for doing what he wanted. And now I was taking off to his pad all of a sudden.

I didn't do "sudden," unless I felt like it.

He stepped into my personal space and nudged a finger under my chin before he dropped his hand. His closeness felt weird. Intimate.

"If you're scared . . ."

I stared into his dark lenses. "I'm not scared."

"Then get in. Nothing bad's gonna happen." He gave a half smile. "Unless you want it to."

Suddenly I felt as if I'd been imported into a dumb teen commercial with the idiot friend peer-pressuring a chug of a beer. Except edit the idiot friend and replace him with a cute guy with brown skin and spiked hair. Voices from behind me diverted my attention. I turned to see Nathan and Misty walking across the parking lot. I hadn't noticed earlier, but Nathan's navy blue Chevy pickup was parked a few slots away.

Nathan's eyes met mine and a funny zing happened in my chest. He'd been smiling at Misty, but when he saw me the smile fell away. Misty walked off to her car and—great—Nathan passed his own, dropping his jock bag into the bed of his truck and making his way straight for us. Miguel and I shifted to face him. Miguel stayed in my personal space for some unexplainable reason.

"Hey, Nathan," I said, filling the uncomfortable silence.

Nathan just looked at Miguel, then me, his thick eyebrows furrowing like he tried to figure out some kind of puzzle. I noticed his hair was damp, probably from a shower after his run.

"Need something, Ramos?" Miguel wanted to know.

I kind of did, too.

Nathan kept his gaze on me. "Need to talk to Angel a minute."

I did my best not to give away a facial reaction, but what was up with two hot guys wanting to talk to me? This didn't happen on a daily basis.

Miguel snorted and jerked his shoulders. "Whatever." He went to slouch on his front seat.

My eyebrows pinched in annoyance. "Hold on. I think I get a say in this." Sure, I wouldn't pass up the opportunity to hang out with Nathan, but for Miguel—or anyone for that matter—to assume Nathan needed his permission was straight ignorant.

Nathan shook his head. "Sorry. Walk with me to my ride?" He gave an encouraging smile.

That was a little more like it. We walked slowly and stopped by the passenger door of Nathan's pickup. His back to Miguel, mine to his truck. Nathan was an entire head taller than me, but over Nathan's shoulder I could still see Miguel watching us. I acted like I didn't notice.

I met Nathan's eyes. "What's up?"

Nathan slipped his hands in his front pockets and leaned his weight on his left foot. His white shirt was a little loose, but somehow stretched around his shoulders. His skin looked nicely bronzed against the fabric. "What are you doing with Badalin, Angel?"

"What?" Yeah, I'd heard him. It's just that I really hadn't expected this question. Maybe something about art class? The presentation? Anything other than something . . . personal. We'd managed to keep it light between us for two years.

"Why are you with him?"

I shook my head as if I still didn't get his question. I guess I didn't. "The obvious. Hanging out. Why?"

"He's bad news."

I shrugged. "So he ditches class. Who doesn't?"

His eyebrows lowered over his eyes. "You have to know he does more than that."

I released the shoulder straps on my pack and stuffed my hands in the front pocket of my pullover. No, actually, I didn't know all that much about Miguel, but I didn't say it out loud because Nathan's annoyed tone pissed me off. Funny thing, my mother had always taught me any kind of attention from the guy you liked was better than none at all, but guess what? I just didn't feel the same way. I could already feel my body language going slack, my expression saying, *Like I care what you think*. A real instant reaction.

"What's it to you who I hang out with, anyway?" I hit back at him.

"Let's just say I'm trying to return the favor for you standing up for my sister, Yoli, last summer."

I looked down at the asphalt and kicked a small rock. Yeah, the flag football game here on the field. Beth wanted to check out the shirtless guys. A girl and her friend had been sitting on the sideline and a few older girls from a gang had started messing with them, throwing garbage at the girls' heads. I wasn't the type to go looking for trouble, especially with a gang, but the girls had looked scared out of their freaking minds. So I'd stepped in because I'd known one of the *chicas* and was pretty sure I wouldn't get my ass beat. I hadn't known one of them was Nathan's little sister at the time.

The fact that Nathan felt he owed me something more

than the thanks he gave then irritated me. I lifted my head and shrugged. "I don't need any returned favors."

He looked away, a twitch flexing his jaw. "If that's the way you feel."

"Yeah . . . just forget about it. I already did."

A small sarcastic smile curved his mouth. "All right. Guess Badalin's waiting." He still wouldn't meet my eyes so I straightened my shoulders and walked away.

Back to someone who did show a little more interest.

Miguel Badalin.

chapter **three**

DOWN
To Be Accepted Within a Group and
Be Cool with Them.

—Angel's Piecebook Notes

(Something that seemed to be happening to me.)

Miguel drove us away from NHH while listening to Bone Thugs-N-Harmony. His favorite band, which he was convinced would start touring again, Bizzy included. Not that Miguel talked much, unlike Derek the blab mouth.

Well, both Derek and Beth.

Apparently they were hitting it off, dishing out North Homestead gossip and flirtatiously arguing with each other.

"Yeah, right. Who told you that?"

"A friend of a friend."

"No way it's true."

"I'm telling you, there were pictures."

I remained silent. Thinking. What had been up with Nathan?

I'd never seen him act so . . . I couldn't even think of the right word . . . intense, bossy—just not himself. But then, maybe that was his real self. I'd only seen the jokester side to him.

And also the quiet side, like when he was into his artwork. His expression focused on his creation, not caring what anyone thought. To tell you the truth, a guy who walked his own road appealed to me. Nathan was that kind of a guy when it came to his art.

I blinked his image away. He wasn't the senior I was with at the moment.

Yeah, the fact that Miguel was that same kind of guy wasn't lost on me, either.

Miguel cut the engine. The pounding music shut off so quickly the silence was shocking. The next sound was the clatter of his shades hitting the dash, followed by the shifting of bodies as we each climbed out, leaving our stuff in his Blazer. He lived in what looked like a simple, beige two-story patio home, with a neat patch of lawn. A cleaner neighborhood compared to my own, where the houses could use a fresh coat of paint and the lawns were either overgrown or dead. We didn't go inside, though. Miguel stuck a key into a keyhole next to the garage door and the door rose with a low mechanical hum.

I expected to see a basic empty shell of a garage. A washer and dryer sat by a door that entered into the house, but that was where the "basic" ended.

It was like a modern-day Eric Forman hangout from *That '70s Show*.

Two worn couches, a television on an old file cabinet topped with an Xbox, and in front of it sat an ancient coffee table with scarred edges scattered with games and a couple of video controllers. But what was really cool was the art displayed everywhere.

The graffiti art.

So the rumors are true . . .

Not just spray painted names, what I knew were called "tags"—although there was an entire mass of them on the right wall—but elaborate colorful designs painted in Miguel's in-your-face style. One center design on the left wall depicted three *cholo* characters wearing baggy pants and buttoned-up flannels. Their hands were stuffed in their pockets, bandannas tied low on the foreheads. Painted in silver and black beside the characters was *"Reyes del Norte."* North Kings.

"Wow," Beth said as we stepped into the dim halogen-lit area.

A musty scent mixed with a faint chemical odor reached my nose. "Your parents let you do this?" I asked.

"Yeah, my pops." Sounded like there was no mom in the picture. At this house, anyway.

I heard a soft flick and turned to see Miguel lighting a cigarette. The tip flared and then he exhaled. The scent of smoke reached me. He lifted the pack in my direction. Marlboro Reds.

Taking one, I placed the soft filter between my lips. He offered a black lighter toward me and lit the tip.

Inhaling too much, I experienced the burn at the back of my throat and then blew out smoke. Immediately I felt a little lightheaded. I was used to the Marlboro Lights I sometimes snagged from my mom's pack. The pack she hid in her underwear drawer and swore she didn't have.

"Flick the ashes in that can over there."

There was an old coffee can atop a wall shelf, so I took another drag and tapped my ash in.

I pinched the cigarette between my thumb and fingers and moved to the left wall. Beside the *cholo* design was another creation painted in erratic green and blue lines, tubes, and arrows. The edges were smooth and clean, the colors fading into one another. I realized the faint chemical odor was spray paint. Couldn't quite make out what the design said, but I knew it spelled something.

"Do you like it?"

Miguel's voice so close made me flinch. I turned to him.

He looked directly into my eyes, like somehow my answer was important. It was the first time I noticed how thick his eyelashes were.

I answered honestly. "Yeah, it's cool."

"Know what it says?"

I let out a short laugh. "No idea."

He took my free hand and pulled me back, his grip warm. "You're too close."

I took my hand back when we reached the other side of the garage, but then he swung an arm over my shoulders, his body not completely touching mine.

I automatically tensed. Obviously I wasn't used to being "touchy-feely" with him since I just started talking with him today. But I didn't move away. It wasn't totally uncool, just a new and different feeling to be close to him.

"Look at it. You're an artist, you see shapes in objects others don't."

My lips curved. Having someone call me an artist was rare and good to hear. After a moment the colors of the design formed a pattern. The arrows aimed in a certain direction for a purpose.

I took another hit of the smoke. "Looks like bad . . . man. Badman."

"Give the *chica* another cigarette. Or how 'bout a Coke?" He released me, flicked his cigarette in the can, and walked to a minifridge, then tossed us each a soda.

Beth frowned. "I don't see it."

Well, I could. Badman. Badalin. He made his tag name close to his last name. I couldn't remember seeing the tag around town anywhere, though.

Derek fell onto one of the couches. The sound of old springs followed. He grabbed the remote from the coffee table and clicked on the TV like he owned the place. "Probably because you're *not* an artist."

Beth strolled to the couch and sat on the other end. She settled more quietly. "Oh, and you are?"

Not in the mood to be witness to another teasing debate, I turned away and finished off the cigarette, letting the heated smoke roll across my tongue and out my mouth. Then I tossed the butt in the makeshift ashtray and opened the tab of my drink.

"Angel, come on," Miguel said. "I'll show you my piecebook."

"Yeah, Beth," Derek blabbed in a tone that surely insinuated he was a perv. "And I'll show you my piecebook, too, any time you want to see it."

"Yeah, right!"

"Piecebook?" I asked, ignoring them both and following Miguel to the door that led into the house.

"Like a sketchbook." He held the door open for me. The entry led into a kitchen with granite counters and dark brown cupboards. A small dining area was next to it with a square table and four chairs. Nothing adorning the table or the kitchen walls. Nana always had something on each wall in our house so this kitchen looked sterile to me.

I glanced back at Beth. She and Derek were sitting next to each other. When had they gotten so close?

"Only be a minute," Miguel said.

I scraped my foot across the concrete floor. "Hey, just bring it out here."

He smirked. "Scared, aren't you?"

"Whatever." The gist of it was, I just didn't know Miguel that well yet. Yeah, we had a class together, and the guy was definitely hot. Big freaking deal. I had class with lots of people. Didn't mean I was their friend or knew how they lived behind closed doors . . . or that I wanted to find out.

He smiled, shook his head. "So cautious." He disappeared into the house.

I shrugged, knowing he was right. I didn't always follow the rules, but there were things in life you couldn't always trust. Something I first learned in second grade at Tanya Martinez's house. Her older brother, Antonio, who was a sixth grader at the time, had pulled me into his room, held tightly onto my head, and pushed his mouth against mine. I'd tried to pull away, but the jerk was too strong. The fear that had rushed through me that this kid was bigger, stronger, and forcing me to do something I didn't want to do was an incident I'd never forget. Even now I managed to get goose bumps from the memory. Luckily, I managed to kick him hard enough for him to let me go. Too bad I missed between his legs.

I never did tell Nana or Mom—maybe because no one ever asked—but it wasn't likely anyone would ask a kid if another kid had tried to force a tongue down her throat. So yeah, I was usually cautious being alone with people I didn't know well, sometimes too much. I went with what felt right and skipped what felt wrong. Call it following my instincts.

Beth and Derek quieted down as I parked myself on the other couch. Gee, was I interrupting something?

A few more Latino guys strolled up to the garage, some I'd seen around school hanging out with Miguel. One of them was the kid who had come with him to art class earlier today. They started talking with Derek. Now that I thought about it, they were all juniors, too. Didn't Miguel have any friends from his grade?

Beth came and sat next to me.

"So you and Miguel, huh?" she whispered.

I shook my head. "No."

"Then why are we here?"

"Remember? The artwork?"

"That's it?"

Looking into her blue eyes, I nearly told her this wasn't *The Real World* where everyone jonesed to hook up, but I didn't want to hurt her feelings. Beth was cool and she stuck with me no matter what, but sometimes it bothered me that she didn't get my art. How much it really was a part of me. Beth's perspective with creativity didn't ever go farther than the surface. I knew I had to realize there were people who just didn't connect with art—like my mom—and accept it, yet it was always hard for me to do. I guess that was why I was here at the house of a guy I hardly knew. Art crossed boundaries and connected people who normally wouldn't hang out to-gether.

Miguel finally came back out with a couple of books in his hand. He started doing those "guy" handshakes with his friends, clasping hands, sliding into curling fingers, then knocking their hands together.

Beth and I set our cans on the table and stood up. Miguel introduced us to all of them.

There was Petey with the bleached dyed spikes, Mateo, who was a skinny kid with a skateboard, and a big, stocky guy with a shaved head who went by the name Rock.

I nodded my head toward them. "How's it going? Look, we have to go."

"Already?" Miguel asked.

I rolled a shoulder. "Plans." Wasn't really a lie. Just sounded better than saying I had to get home and finish my homework. Keeping this 3.0 average wasn't easy.

"Check these out first."

He sat down on the couch, opening a black hardcover sketchbook. I joined him, with Beth looking over my shoulder.

The first page was filled with a colorful, intricate design like that on his garage wall. "Badman, Crew RDN" written underneath. The next drawing spelled out "BADMAN." The following pages had characters wearing a bandanna low over their eyes, arms crossed, leaning against the word. Another sketch was of odd-looking characters with spiky hair, a couple that spelled out "*Reyes del Norte.*" I was impressed by the cleanliness of the design and the colors that grabbed your attention and held it. The designs were bold and brash, layered with different colors and textures. Some were even actual stickers of graffiti-style words slapped crookedly on the page. This art definitely made a statement.

"These are awesome," I said, and Beth agreed.

"Bet you could do this," he said.

I shook my head. "No way, Jack."

"You could do that, Angel," Beth encouraged.

Miguel turned the pages, showing more characters with exaggerated feet and spray cans in their hands. "Takes practice. You already have the cartoon style that would be cool for pieces like these."

I let my irritation roll off me. I didn't want to have this whimsical style. I wanted to be better. More realistic.

"This is how I learned." He handed me a book titled *Crazy Wild Styles.* "You practice by drawing from examples, then you put your own spin on the designs. You can borrow it for a while, if you want." He pointed to my shoes. "Looks like you're heading in the right direction."

I gazed down at the character faces I'd drawn with dark Sharpie ink on my K-Swisses. When I looked up, our heads were close. Close enough I could see his eyes were solid brown with no other color mixed in. Not dark brown like chocolate, but an almost golden brown like . . . honey.

"I like how you focus on Latino culture in your work," he said. "We need more artists expressing our way of life, you know? An artist just has to find the right kind of art that calls to him. Graffiti could be for you."

I could feel myself frowning because I wanted to ask why he was even showing me all this stuff, but not with all the guys around.

"Eh, don't think too hard." He smiled. "Come on, I'll give you guys a ride home."

I lifted a hand as Miguel drove off and strolled onto the cracked walkway toward my two-bedroom house. The front lawn was overgrown, mixed with dry and barely green grass. Mom never did yardwork. She said being on her feet for ten-hour shifts and having to do house cleaning was enough. Nana was plagued with painful arthritis in her back from years of working in the agricultural fields and walked with a cane most days. Every so often I took the hose to the lawn, but I forgot most of the time. Yardwork wasn't a priority. I looked over at the two adjoining neighbors' lawns. Seemed like they pretty much had the same outlook. So why worry about it myself?

Settling my pack and portfolio case on the lawn, I slipped my hands into my sweatshirt and backtracked to the sidewalk. Around the corner, I stepped onto the small sand area of North Caesar Park. Two Latino boys sat atop the steel dome, dangling their legs in the air. I grabbed one of the three swings and sat for a moment, gripping the hard chains in my hands.

I'd been coming to this park since I was three years old, had played on that dome structure, swung on these swings, and slid down that same slide, which was still the original structure of wood and steel. Nothing had changed. Even when new parks had been built with plastic and steel, and parks in richer neighborhoods upgraded, North Caesar stayed the same. Gang signatures scored the bottom of the slide and the brick walls by the single basketball court. The walls I hoped would be part of the mural community project and be painted with art depicting the town's Latino culture. Maybe painted by my own hand.

So yeah, this was my park. My neighborhood. I didn't want it overhauled, but was wanting it cleaned up a little too much to ask? Was being part of its changes too much to hope for?

I shoved those thoughts aside because sometimes wishes hurt too much when they don't come true. And like I did every few days, I checked to see if anyone was looking, then walked around the sandbox and collected a few pieces of glass, a bottle, and a wrinkled cigarette pack and dumped them in the dented garbage can before returning home.

I grabbed my stuff and was just about to climb up the two cemented steps to our front door when I heard the squeak of worn car brakes behind me. Turning, I blew out a breath at the sight of the familiar maroon Cadillac. José, my mom's recent ex-boyfriend. The Capricorn mechanic with the blood-shot eyes. That's how I'd come to label them—by astrological sign, occupation, and some distinct feature that stood out. Before him there had been the Gemini plumber with the overbite. The Scorpio bartender with a lisp. And I couldn't forget the Taurus minimart manager with the giant mole on his forehead.

My mom wasn't home at this time of day. José knew this, so coming around now meant he'd likely been drinking and having one of those he-wanted-Monica-back moments, and not even sober enough to realize what he was doing. Unfortunately, I'd been a witness to similar moments with Mom's ex-boyfriends before, and they never got easier.

José slowly slid out of his car and slammed the door shut. He wore a greased white T-shirt and those navy blue work-pants mechanics often wore and black steel-toed boots. His hair was a black mass atop his head, his eyebrows dark, his eyes bloodshot.

He stopped about three feet away from me. "Your *mamá* home, Angelita?"

"She's working. I'll tell her you came by." I took a step and reached for the black, metal screen door.

"How is she, Angelita?"

"My name's Angel," I said, knowing it was a waste of breath.

"She won't return my calls. She won't talk to me when I try at her work. *Por qué*? Tell me."

My shoulders started that steady tightening they did when I got upset. I didn't know the exact reason Mom dumped him. Didn't care. He'd been around two long months before my mom came to her senses and finally realized he was another lowlife. What the hell did he want from me? The truth? That I was glad she dumped his sorry ass before he weaseled a cheap ring on her finger?

"I don't know."

He took a step closer and latched onto my arm.

My heartbeat flickered hard in my chest. A funny prickling started on the back of my head. I automatically tugged against his grip, but he held tight. My portfolio case dangled between us. *"Step off."*

"I love her. Will you tell her I want her back? I need her." The sour odor of beer drifted from his breath, his fingers digging into my forearm.

"I'll tell her, all right? *Get lost.*" The front door opened behind the screen door and I finally yanked my arm free from his grip.

"Angel?" Nana said.

José was already walking away. I pulled open the screen and slammed it at my back. My shoulders were moving up and down fast. I swallowed to build up saliva in my dry mouth. I shut my eyes and willed myself to calm down. *He's gone. Everything's fine.*

When my breath settled, I realized I was holding onto my portfolio case as if it were a lifeline, and that Nana stood beside me looking at me with concerned dark eyes.

"What did he want, *m'ija*?"

The familiar anger flashed hot inside me. I threw my portfolio case on our yellow paisley couch, following with my pack. I shook my head. "What do you think, Nana? He wants Mom back. Just like all the other stupid boyfriends she falls for." What was it with my mom that she couldn't see jerks for what they were?

Ignoring my throbbing arm, I stalked past a rerun of *Family Feud* playing on the television to the kitchen, taking in the warm scents of *pozole* cooking on the stove. Pulling open the refrigerator, I grabbed the water jug and pulled off the cap, raising the bottle toward my mouth.

"*M'ija*, a glass, *por favor*."

Releasing a breath, I did as she asked.

A round of applause erupted from the television in the front room and Nana craned her neck to see. "I bet you it was that family from Kansas," she murmured, then louder, "*Tu mamá* is looking for the right man, *m'ija*." Nana walked with her wooden cane to the kitchen table, her aged dark hand grasping the cane's brass handle.

Right. My mom had been looking for seventeen years. But I didn't say that out loud. I treated Nana with respect, always had. She took good care of me and was there when I needed her. I tried not to take out my frustrations on her. I saved that for the person who deserved it.

Nana sighed. "I think she's looking for a man to match the integrity of her *papá*."

My grandfather had passed away a year before I was born.

Nana always spoke highly of him, so I couldn't see how the guys my mom dated could compare. But I knew she spoke the truth. My mom was looking for the right man . . . she just hadn't found him yet. With men like José around, I wondered if she ever would.

I deliberately relaxed my nerves, refraining from rubbing my arm. No need to upset Nana by telling her the idiot had grabbed me. The table was already set for the two of us, and I walked over and poured Nana a glass of water.

"Nana, we can eat in the front room with the TV trays."

"No, no. I want to talk to you. I watch my game shows all day."

It was true. Nana had a near obsession.

After washing our hands, we were both settled with a bowl of soup. Nana's thin lips curved, flashing her one silver capped tooth among an otherwise nice smile. "Tell me. How did the presentation go?"

If it was my mom asking I would have shrugged the question off, but this was Nana. And really, would my mom even ask? "Not so great. Mr. Chun called it 'whimsical.' " I shook my head and combed hair out my face.

"Whimsical is good, *sí*?"

I wouldn't lie to Nana, but I couldn't always share my true feelings. "Let's just say, it's not the greatest."

"You worked hard on the presentation. The judges will see."

I sipped a spoon of broth and hominy for lack of something better to do than say what I really felt. Nana was, well . . . old. She had no idea about today's art society. Had no idea what looked cool and what didn't. I was beginning to think she just had faith in my art because she loved me. And truthfully? Nana's love and faith were great, but I knew her belief in me wasn't going to make my dreams of becoming a respected artist come true.

I'd just finished the last of my homework and Nana was getting ready for bed. I took off the worn cushions from the couch, grabbed the metal handle, and pulled out the mattress. The old metal legs squeaked with the motion. Before I unfolded the bed completely, I brought out the money from my pack I'd made that morning and felt under the couch for my envelope stash. I took out the bills from the envelope and quickly counted what I'd saved. Now I had fifty-one dollars. Time for an art supply run. I folded the money into the envelope and slipped it in a tear in the fabric of the couch inside the thick leg, then finished making my bed.

The pullout couch wasn't the greatest, but it was all I'd known for the past seven years. Mom had gotten pregnant with me while still living in this house with Nana. My biological dad, who was apparently some college white guy vacationing on the West Coast for the summer, was a no-show. As in he got my mom pregnant at sixteen and then returned to college, not ever looking back. Mom had never tried to find him and ever since my grandfather's death all she had was Nana. Nana had two brothers and a horde of cousins, but they were all in Mexico. I'd been sleeping in the front room since I was nine, I had shared a room with my mom before then. That time seemed so far away—back when I would feel her warmth next to mine in bed. Back when she would come home from work smelling like cigarette smoke and sometimes the different food scents from the restaurant where she worked as a waitress.

Our house had drawers set into the hallway walls beneath a cabinet where I kept my clothes and belongings. I changed into sweats and a T-shirt, unbound my hair, then settled on my bed to pull out Miguel's book from my pack. His cute half smile formed in my mind.

You already have the cartoon style that would be cool for pieces like these.

An artist just has to find the right kind of art that calls to him. Graffiti could be for you.

I moved a finger across my bottom lip. *Have I been focusing my energy in the wrong direction?* I opened the book to the first page. A graffiti design was spray painted on the rusted car of a train. Words I could barely read. I ran my finger over the white slanted letters outlined in blue. What kind of artistic future could learning graffiti really bring? If I played by school rules, I'd be part of a cool community project. One day there could be the possibility of junior college.

Did I even want to go to college?

With each page I turned, the designs became bolder and

brasher. The designs were usually on cement walls, or trains, but some were more daring. Graffiti painted at the very top of a twenty-story building. I lifted my eyebrows at a rough design by "DNGR" on an actual police car. Gutsy.

What was so wrong if I learned a new style? It wasn't like I was out for tagging up the town like this book seemed to be about, and I would tell Miguel that upfront. I was just curious about the method, how I could use it to express myself.

That's what these artists were doing. Making a statement. Shouting out to the world that they wanted to be noticed. Respected for their artwork. No doubt, I could relate.

The door to the bathroom opened and I quickly closed the book and slipped it inside my pack. Nana walked into the front room wearing her faded green dress robe, her long salt-and-pepper hair in a braid down her back. *"Buenas noches, m'ija."*

I walked over and hugged her good night. When Nana patted my back and kissed my cheek, I smelled the rose-scented powder she liked to use. Sometimes I felt too old to give her hugs each night before bed, but habits died hard in this house.

"Don't worry about the presentation," she said. "Good things will happen."

"All right, Nana. 'Night."

I went to the bathroom to wash my face and brush my teeth, then walked out to the front room. The black sombrero with bright orange thread sitting on a shelf that Nana had brought home from a long-ago visit to Mexico caught my attention first, followed by the red and yellow Mexican blanket folded over the old green chair. I made my way to the painting on the wall of a Mexicano pulling a burro. Reaching out, I traced my fingers along the textured edges of the oil painting. The soft blends of yellow and blue were excellent, the symbolism of culture and land strong.

Above the signature of the artist at the bottom of the painting, I traced "A. Rodriguez."

"Someday," I said under my breath, and then turned away to climb into bed.

It was late when the front door opened and cold air filtered into the front room. I snuggled deeper into my blankets on the pull-out bed. When I heard my mother whisper and then smother a laugh, I stilled. A male voice whispered something back.

Someone was seeing my mom home from work.

Just one of the sure signs he was yet another *hombre* my mother could give her heart to.

A man who sees you home and walks you to your door is a real man, Angel.

A small span of silence occurred and I knew they were kissing good night. Likely the first kiss. My mom fell hard for a good kisser, too.

She finally said good night and closed and locked the door.

I didn't dare move a muscle until I heard her bedroom door shut.

I waited . . .

When I heard the first muted sounds of Bon Jovi's "I'll Be There for You," I shut my eyes.

Mom was in love. Again.

chapter four

BATTLE
Opposing Writers Piece a Wall
to See Who Can Best Who
        —Angel's Piecebook Notes
        (Others best me a lot.)

a distant beeping sounded in my head. I rolled over in bed, curled deeper into the warm blankets, and ignored it.

"Angel, wake up." A pressure on my shoulder, nudging me. "Come on. It's time to get up for school. Your alarm went off."

I rolled onto my back and managed to open my eyes to a slit. *So freaking tired.* My mom stood above me, next to the pull-out bed. Her long light brown hair was messed up from sleep, a thick burgundy robe wrapped around her. Her eyelids were heavy and her light skin was paler than usual. She got like that when she didn't get enough rest. Yeah, my mom was Mexican-American, but she was light-skinned just like my grandfather had been. I remembered when I was little my friends wouldn't believe my mom was Mexican, even going so far as to wonder if I was adopted because I was about three shades darker than her, more like Nana's coloring.

I rubbed my fingers against the graininess of my eyelids.

"Were you up late again watching MTV?"

"No . . . it was you, and whoever came to the door." I was grouchy enough to start in on her early today.

"Oh. Didn't mean to keep you up." She ran a hand over her face and back through her hair. "Did you see him? What did you think?"

I sat up and swung my legs over the side of the bed, stretched. "Nope, didn't see him. Shucks, maybe next time." I knew I sounded sarcastic but meeting my mom's new boyfriends wasn't exactly a rare occurrence. "Speaking of your love life . . . José was here yesterday."

Her small smile flattened. "When? What did he want?"

"Around dinner. Wanted to know why you dumped him." I stood up. "I think we need to get a dog to keep away the pissed-off jerks you dump." I started past her and she grabbed my arm. I winced, realizing José must have bruised me and yanked my arm away.

"What did he say?"

"I thought you were going back to bed?" I continued on to the bathroom.

"Don't pull attitude on me this early, Angel."

"Always me," I murmured before telling her louder, "He wants you back. He misses you, needs you. Bullshit stuff."

"Watch your mouth!"

"Whatever." My mother and I were pretty hot-tempered. We raised our voices at each other when we became angry or sometimes when we were just emotional, and watch out when we were on our periods. Nana was the only quiet one in the household.

I nearly had the satisfaction of closing the bathroom door in my mom's face when she blocked it with a straight arm.

She met my eyes, hers more alert now. "Is that all that happened?"

"Yes, all right? I didn't know I had to give a full report."

"Next time, don't answer the door. All right, Angel? I mean it."

I frowned, but nodded in agreement.

She dropped her arm and her eyelids went heavy again. "Have a good day at school."

My chest tightened. I swung the door open wider. "That's all you're ever worried about, right? Anything that concerns the ignorant men in your life."

She blew out a frustrated breath, roughly shoving her hair out of her face. "That's not true, and you know it. *Look*, I'm running on three hours of sleep and I have to pull a double shift tonight so one of the girls can stay home with her sick kid. We'll talk later."

"You didn't even ask me how my presentation went." It was out before I could stop it.

She crossed her arms, sighed. "It slipped my mind. How did it go?"

She forgot. She always forgot about my art. "Never mind."

"Oh, Angel. Just tell me."

I snorted. "Why? Because you care?"

"*Mierda*. I do care, Angel, about you!"

"Whatever, just go back to bed." I slammed the door shut and turned the lock, fighting the lump forming in my throat. My stomach began a slow burn right in the center and I felt like screaming. Yet I held it in as I stared at the orange flowers on the plastic shower curtain.

I heard Nana saying something to my mother through the door. My mom's raised voice saying, "She's so stubborn! I don't need this crap so early in the morning!"

I shoved back the shower curtain, just like I shoved aside all thoughts of my mother.

Unexpected things happened all the time. I knew that. Like you could be walking outside and the wind blew a dollar bill across your path when you were hurting for a soda. Or maybe you didn't study that well for a test, but ended up getting an okay grade anyway.

But when I entered Mr. Chun's class on Friday afternoon and read, "We Have a Winner!" scrawled across the ink board, I tried to figure out if this was a good unexpected moment or one that seriously sucked.

How could the school faculty have already come to a decision? The class just turned in the projects twenty-three hours ago.

"That was quick," Nathan said to me.

Serious understatement. I nodded anyway, my fingers creeping toward my mouth.

"Well, everybody," Mr. Chun announced. "As you can see from the board, the faculty came to an early decision."

Forget the dead skin hunt. I crossed my arms against my chest.

"It wasn't an easy choice."

My eyes arrowed straight on him. He stood before the class with a slip of paper in his hand, using his forefinger to push his glasses back up the wide bridge of his nose. And suddenly this hesitation came over me, as if I wasn't all that sure I wanted to know if I'd lost. I'd put so much thought and consideration into this project and to find out my best wasn't good enough . . . would mean *I* wasn't good enough.

Unfortunately, there was no hesitation for Mr. Chun.

"But we managed to narrow it down to three exceptional designs, and finally came to one design that would best represent North Homestead."

I licked my lips and shifted in my seat.

"Second runner up—Miguel Badalin!"

Clapping erupted, and I slowly joined in. I swallowed hard. Could I have beat out Miguel?

Miguel gave a lopsided smile that quickly disappeared, his right knee bouncing. I noticed his fingers gliding up and down on his wallet chain. It didn't seem like he was too happy with his placement.

"First runner up—"

I held my breath.

"Lydia Wesley!"

More clapping.

I locked gazes with Nathan. My heart pounded. Did that mean . . .

"And the head chair of the mural committee—Nathan Ramos!"

My breath expelled out of my mouth in a gush. Nathan beamed a satisfied hundred-watt smile.

I'd lost.

Totally.

Not even a freaking runner-up.

Something hard shifted inside my chest. Somehow I still managed to smile. "Congrats, Nathan. You deserve it."

"Thanks." Something flickered in his eyes. "Hey, sorry . . ."

"Don't be." Lifting a stiff shoulder, I said, "Win some, lose some." In my case . . . I always lost.

Rising to my feet, I walked over to grab one of the wooden rectangle hallway passes off the wall and left the room. I dug my fingers into the smooth texture of the wood. No, I didn't want to look like the loser who ran off to be alone, but if I stayed around I was more afraid of disappointment showing on my face.

Heat warmed my cheeks. I picked up my pace to the girls' bathroom. Shoving open the door, the funky bathroom stink hit my nostrils, but I didn't care. I paused to listen. No movement. I was alone. I leaned back against the mint-colored tiled wall and slowly sank to the cold floor, resting my folded arms on my bent knees, my forehead hitting my arms, my hands fisted tight.

A lump burned my throat, but no way in hell would I cry here, in the smelly girls' bathroom where anyone could see the evidence of humiliation on my face. That's not how I worked. I held in my pain like a dirty secret, swallowing past the thickness.

How could I have been so stupid? Thinking I'd actually had a chance of winning just because I'd worked my ass off on the presentation. Yeah, like effort had anything to do with result. But for some reason I had held on to this little piece of hope . . .

Someone came in and I lifted my head, schooling my expression to pissed off. It was the easiest emotion to show right now. A freshman looked at me, then quickly looked away before she locked herself into a stall the color of dark pink puke.

I heard the door swing open again. "Angel Rodriguez, you in there?" a familiar male voice echoed in the room.

Great. I scrubbed my hands across my face and stood.

"Yeah, I'm here." I pulled the elastic from my head, walked to the mirror, and pulled all my hair back, wrapping the band around my mass of hair.

"You alone?" Miguel asked.

"No. Don't come in, all right?" I didn't want the little freshman to freak out or anything.

Miguel's laughter echoed against the tiled walls.

The toilet flushed and the freshman hurried and washed her hands, her face reddening, as she rushed out the door.

I stepped in front of the entryway. Miguel stood there holding the door open, wearing a crooked grin, the other class hallway pass sticking out of his baggy jean pocket. He cocked his head as he looked at me. He was kinda cute when he did that. "You gonna stay in there all day?"

Actually, that would have been just fine with me if I could have gotten away with it. I stepped out into the hallway. We started back to class.

"So what? You're upset you didn't win?"

I didn't answer. "Congrats on placing in the finals. Now you have a guaranteed spot on the committee."

"They weren't gonna pick somebody like me as the winner. Just the school's all-star pretty boy."

I snuck a quick look at him. What the hell did Nathan and Miguel have against each other?

"I passed on the committee," he said. "Wasn't for me."

My eyebrows rose. "You did?" Why had he put so much effort into his design then?

He nodded. "Besides, Ramos probably didn't even draw that design on his own. I didn't want to be a part of something rigged."

I stopped and swiveled in front of him. "Whatever. That presentation had Nathan written all over it."

He turned, his mouth suddenly in a flat line, and gripped my lower arm tighter than I liked, as if trying to force me somewhere.

I frowned, pulling free. "What the hell, Badalin?"

He stared at me for a long uncomfortable moment, then blew out a breath and went to lean his shoulder against some lockers. It was clear he wanted me to follow. I stood there for a couple of seconds, then gave in to my curiosity and did the same, facing him.

"Angel, listen," he said, his eyes meeting mine. "Ramos gave Mr. Chun the names he wanted on the committee."

I nodded. I was so close to him, I could smell the cologne he was wearing. I tried to tell myself it wasn't nice.

"He chose you."

My eyes narrowed. "What?"

"Yeah, he chose you for the committee." He straightened, looked down at the floor a second, then back to my gaze. "I feel bad telling you this, but you should know."

I searched his face. Why did I get the impression he was about to lay out some bad news? "Go ahead. Just spill it."

"Nah, I don't know. Forget it."

He couldn't just say that, then tell me to forget it. That

was like waving an entire box of brand new Prisma pencils in front of me, then taking them away. "Whatever." I pulled away from the locker and turned to leave.

"All right, damn. Hold up, *chica*."

I faced him again, giving him a look that said I couldn't care less if he told me one way or the other. Putting up a front was one of my specialties.

"Yesterday when you were giving your presentation in class, Nathan said he knew you wouldn't win. That he'd choose you to be on the committee because he felt sorry for you."

I shook my head. "You're lying." Like Nathan would ever confide in him.

"Eh, I'm not." He held up his hands as if he could push away my doubts. "I told him nobody wants his work to be put down like that—pitied or something—but he didn't care. He said you weren't good enough to even get on the committee without him. But he knew you had a crush on him, and he didn't want your feelings hurt or some shit."

A sense of unease tiptoed under my skin. That sounded like Nathan, all right, thinking about other people's feelings. Worried I'd be upset because I didn't win. I had seen Nathan and Miguel talking during my presentation.

He knows I like him?

I hadn't thought I could feel any lower. I'd been flat-ass wrong. My first instinct was to save face. "I don't have a crush on him. He's just a friend."

"Who cares what he thinks. He's nobody. I see your talent, Angel."

"So you've said," I spoke quietly, staring at the shoulder of his black tee. The hem of the sleeve was loose, but you could also see that he had muscle beneath the fabric. "I don't know. You could just be saying that like . . . him."

"There's one thing you should know. I think someone sucks, I'm straight. I tell 'em. I'm not the nicest guy."

Probably had a point there. Truthfully, I didn't know what to think right now.

"I told you before, your style would be awesome for graf pieces. With your Latino art, you could be a damn graffiti powerhouse. I could teach you. If you have a unique style, that's what makes your art stand out, that's what makes you somebody."

Bull's-eye. It was like my focus zeroed in on him completely for the first time since he found me in the restroom.

His serious eyes held an intensity that could be perceived as passion and truth. Something that made me want to be around him, as if a little of that something could rub off on me.

. . . that's what makes your art stand out.

"What do you say?" he asked, his voice lowered. Intimate.

I stared into his dark eyes. What did I have to lose? I'd already lost the mural competition. But the fact was . . . I might be on the committee and it would take a serious effort to keep up my grades while making time to attend the mural meetings.

I wouldn't even have much time to learn graffiti. "You know, I'm not into the tagging the town part . . ."

"First off, a tagger and a graffiti artist are completely different. Graffiti is what you make of it."

He was so serious when he spoke about graffiti, like it was important to him.

"We can start this weekend," Miguel added, sweetening the deal.

Maybe it was up to me to make the time. "Let me think about it."

Nathan tapped me on the shoulder on the way out of art class. "Talk to you for a minute?"

I almost said no, since supposedly he knew I liked him and all, but it was kind of hard to avoid the guy when I sat across from him every day. "Sure." We moved to the right side of the hallway.

"Can I get your phone number?"

My stomach fluttered. "Um—"

"For the committee. In case Monday's meeting gets canceled or something."

"Right." Why else would he want my number? I lifted a shoulder, playing like it didn't matter. And it *didn't*. "I guess." I opened my pack and tore off a piece of paper from my notebook. Nathan handed me the graphic pencil with a black soft grip he always had with him. I wrote the digits on the paper with my name and tore it off.

He took my number and the pencil, tucking them both in his back pocket. "Cool. Catch you later."

I cleared my throat. "Hey, Nathan?"

His eyebrows rose.

Great, my cheeks were warming. Whether he thought I had talent or not—whether or not he knew I liked him—somehow it felt necessary to thank him for getting me on the committee. Because he was giving me an opportunity that meant more to me than he knew. "I just wanted to say, thanks."

He nodded. He knew what I was talking about. "You deserve it, Angel. You would have placed . . ."

"What?"

He sighed, then took a step closer to me and lowered his voice. "It sucks, but if you hadn't added Mexican culture to your design, you would have placed."

I stepped back. "You don't know that."

"Actually, I do."

Yeah, right. I said as much with a look.

"A girl I know works in the office. She overheard the faculty meeting and told me this morning. A couple of teachers liked your style, but felt the Mexican emphasis dominated the Viking theme. And because of the diversity of our school, they didn't want us appearing as a Latino school."

"Are you kidding? It doesn't matter that our principal is Mexican and practically half our student body has some form of Latino background?"

My voice held attitude because I was ticked off. I could have kicked my own butt for blowing my chances. But then, I had to be me, not someone others wanted me to be. "So you already knew you'd win before Chun announced it."

He gave me my own look of disbelief back. "No way. She didn't overhear who'd won, just the designs they were talking about."

"Yeah, well." If the faculty had liked my style, I would have at least made third. "Doesn't matter now."

"You deserve to be on the committee." He met my eyes. "Really, Angel."

I scanned his face, unsure if he was hedging or not. Damn, did he really feel sorry for me? Unfortunately, I didn't know whether to believe him or Miguel. But I couldn't stop wanting his statement to be true, or wanting to be on the committee. I wanted to be able to express myself with my art and also make a difference at my community park. I knew I would do all I could to earn my spot.

"All right," he said. I couldn't really say what showed on my face—uncertainty or disbelief? Whatever it was he just smiled and reached out, moving a strand of hair from my cheek. "See you Monday." He walked away.

I released a quiet breath, nearly raising a hand to touch my cheek where his finger accidentally brushed. It had been the first time he'd ever touched me. And the tingling in my chest felt . . . weird.

"He's so freaking *hot*."

I turned to Beth and smiled. "Tell me about it." We started toward our lockers.

"Too bad he's got a girlfriend."

"It doesn't matter. We're just friends."

"Hey," Beth said. "Derek invited us to a party tonight."

"Us? Don't you mean you?"

She hooked her hair behind her ear. "No, I mean *us*. Miguel and his friends are going, too. Miguel will pick us up."

"I take it you already said yes."

She waved her apple green lollipop. "Hell, yeah."

"Whose party?"

"I don't know, but it'll be something to do. He'll pick us up at my house around nine. You can spend the night."

Beth didn't have a curfew. Her parents were divorced and she lived with her mom, who was pretty laid-back. My mom and I had never really settled on what time I had to be home on the weekends. So I just spent the night at Beth's in order to avoid answering twenty questions.

Plus, to be honest, it would be interesting to hang out some more with Miguel. You know, to find out more about graffiti. I nodded. "Cool."

"Ow," I said.

Beth squinted her eyes close to my head, handling tweezers like a pro. "Just a couple more."

"Damn," I hissed as she pulled out two more hairs from my eyebrow. "Enough."

She grinned.

I narrowed my eyes. "Don't even laugh."

She tipped her head back and, yeah, laughed. I halfheartedly shoved at her hip. When she was finished with her amusement at my expense, she stood in front of her dresser mirror to apply her mascara. "If you didn't go so long between plucking, it wouldn't hurt so much."

I shrugged and fell back on her baby blue comforter. "I forget." Besides, I rarely made it a point to look good for a guy. I frowned. I lifted my hands and looked at the faint dark hairs on my knuckles. "I'm so hairy, anyway, I don't think my eyebrows make much difference."

"You have these great thick eyebrows that arch, Angel. Believe me, it makes a difference."

Beth started to apply eyeliner. Sometimes I wondered why Beth wasn't an actual glamour girl like those at our school. She knew all these makeup tricks to make her eyes look bigger and her cheeks rounder, but still dressed all kick-back like me.

"Are you excited about hanging out with Miguel?" she asked.

"I guess. I really want to learn more about graffiti, you know?"

"Yeah." She made a point of looking at me with a big smile. "And it doesn't hurt he's fine to look at, either."

I smiled. "Nope."

A knock sounded on her bedroom door before it opened. "Bethany?"

Beth rolled her eyes as she spun toward the door. "Mom, at least wait until I say 'come in.' "

"Honestly, Bethany. Are you guys leaving soon?"

"In about a half hour, why?"

"I have company coming over so be sure to make yourself scarce. Soon." Then she was gone, closing the door with a hard click.

Beth made a face at the door. "God, I can't even stay in my own house."

"Who's she seeing now?"

"Some customer from the bank. That's where she meets most of them."

I sat up on the bed, my fingers pitching at the soft fabric. "Does it bother you? The different guys she brings home?"

She shook her head. "They leave me alone, so I don't really care. Hey, can you put on some music?"

I walked over to her small boom box on the floor and began sorting through her CDs. This was where Beth and I were so different. It grated that my mom showed more interest in the guys she dated than in me most of the time. Beth was always saying how she thought I looked good or liked the way my thick eyebrows arched, stuff that was on the outside of me. Stuff that didn't matter in my eyes. What Beth didn't know was that I envied stuff about her, too. I wished I didn't care who my mom dated, either.

chapter five

BURN

To Beat the Competition with Your Style
            –Angel's Piecebook Notes
            (Everybody gets burned once in a while.)

The party took place up on The Hill, which was basically another term for the rich—a territory of Homestead that consisted of huge homes, lavish yards, swimming pools, and five-car garages. A place where people from my neighborhood were hired to do landscaping and housekeeping. I was squished in the backseat next to Beth, who was squished next to Rock and Petey. Derek rode shotgun and Mateo sat in the rear storage area. Bone Thugs was booming so loud, the seat vibrated under my butt.

Beth had talked me into wearing my hair down. It reached the middle of my back these days. I really needed a haircut. Beth had run some mousse through it, which brought the waves out, and I'd swiped on some mascara. I wore my low-hip black cargo pants, my K-Swisses, and a long-sleeved purple top with a monkey giving the middle finger. My mom hated this shirt.

Miguel had actually looked at me strange before I stepped into his backseat. So yeah, I knew I looked different, kind of pretty, I guessed. Looking pretty wasn't something I usually thought about or tried to do, but maybe I hoped he liked what he saw tonight. Sometimes Friday nights brought out different attitudes in people. It was the night you could relax after a long week at school, without any adults to answer to. Without caring about anything, but hanging out. Maybe flirting with a cute guy.

Miguel turned into this long, winding driveway and I caught my first glimpse of the three-story house at the end, with every window lit up like bright beacons in the night. Cars were parked everywhere, in front of the house and on the lawn. Miguel found a spot by some kind of fountain— yeah, some fancy fish spitting out water from the mouth— and cut the engine.

"Whose party is this?" I asked no one in particular.

"A college guy named Mark Billings," Petey said from the opposite end of the backseat.

We all got out. I slipped my hands into the front pocket

of my pants out of habit. Beth crossed her arms over her curvy chest. She did that a lot around strangers, I'd noticed.

Music blared out of the open front door. Two older guys hung out in the doorway holding plastic beer cups. They were dressed in baggy pants and sweatshirts. One guy wore a beanie, the other a ball cap on backward. Miguel seemed to know them. He did the hand slap, fist knock handshake.

The guys ran their eyes down Beth and me as if we were fresh meat and yeah, we really didn't belong here. Luckily when we hit the main room, there were other girls there. Some were our age, some older, all of different nationalities. But what I noticed was that the majority of the partygoers were what some kids labeled as skaters. It was the style of clothing they wore: loose attire, solid colors, and bright logos. Except all these clothes were brand spankin' new without a rag shirt in sight. Heads were either shaved or overgrown hair dyed a colorful hue.

A tall guy with brown hair and two-inch goatee, wearing dark pants and a blue tee with a lightbulb printed on the front, came over to Miguel. "What's up, dawg?" They did more guy handshakes. "Keg's in the kitchen, bud's in the backyard." When he said "bud," somehow I knew he wasn't talking beer. "Designer friends hangin' around."

I turned to Beth but she was already walking away with Derek, his arm hooked over her shoulder. She gave me a quick glance, smiled with a shrug, then turned away.

Irritation flickered inside me. We always hung together

at parties when we hardly knew anyone. But I guess she felt she knew Derek and was about to get to know him better. Great.

The other guys followed them, I assumed to the beer. I turned back to Miguel, thinking I would tag along, when the tall guy asked, "Who's this?"

"Angel, this is Mark. He taught me some of what I know about graf."

Mark smiled. "Some, I like that."

"Eh, I'm mostly self-taught."

"You were a toy when I met you."

"Fuck that."

"What's a toy?" I asked.

"Somebody who calls himself a graf writer, but just plays and pretends to be one," Mark said.

My eyebrows lifted. "Cool." I was more than a little surprised that this Mark guy was white. He didn't look Latino at all, although he could just be light-skinned like my mom. I had the impression that Miguel was all about "Brown Pride" when it came to who he created artwork with. But then I didn't know all that much about Miguel.

"You write, Angel?" Mark wanted to know.

". . . write?"

"He's talking about graf," Miguel said to me. Then to Mark, "She wants to learn."

I glanced at Miguel. He and I weren't even clear on how far I wanted to take this, so how could I answer Mark?

Mark looked at Miguel. "Maybe she wants to see some of my work."

Miguel stared at Mark for a moment, then hooked a finger through a belt loop of my pants, tugging me closer to him. "Don't think so."

"All right, then," Mark said and smiled, nearly laughing.

Instinct had me grabbing Miguel's hand and nudging his finger away, but he caught my fingers within his. I didn't look into his eyes. We were standing too close, and for some reason I didn't want to know what he was thinking. I just pushed his hand aside and turned away.

So maybe I'd wanted to flirt a little with Miguel tonight, but it was my choice. No one would make it for me. I wasn't an idiot. Miguel had pretty much called dibs on me. I didn't know whether to blab "Yeah right, Jack" or punch his face.

Behind my back, I heard Mark finally let out that laugh and say something like, "Guess she don't feel the same way, Badalin."

Mark obviously caught on quick.

Miguel didn't follow when I walked away. Smart move. I didn't feel like asking him what the hell was up with that finger-in-the-pant-loop move, or explain my reaction. Unfortunately after about twenty minutes of searching the first floor of the massive house, I couldn't find Beth anywhere. A few people hung out on the staircase all the way up to the second floor, but I didn't go up. With most parties the upstairs usually consisted of the make-out rooms. I seriously hoped I wouldn't have to go searching for Beth up there.

I made my way past leather furniture draped with teenagers sipping from beer cups, and entered the massive kitchen. A group of guys were lined up at the table, counting to three and then starting to drink a line of tequila shots. I walked out the back sliding door.

After the heat of the house, the cold air made me shiver. I crossed my arms against the chill. The back area was huge. It led out to a fancy deck, with, of course, a pool and Jacuzzi. Surprisingly, no one was messed up enough to go swimming in cold weather. Yet. I walked around the curved deck, trying not to gawk. But it was amazing to see what money could buy—an outdoor kitchen, in this case. A large grill with connecting silver counters. A serving bar adjoined by an entire patio of chairs and tables with spiffy white umbrellas.

I imagined adult parties with more elegant guests than the kids hanging out now. People in fancy clothes with snobby names like Charles and Alexis, holding champagne glasses and mingling like the rich did. I didn't think anything else could surprise me about this house until I caught sight of an area past the grass, down cemented steps and a dirt slope. Huge wooden boards were propped up by poles sticking out of the ground, with hordes of kids around them. Another pole with a light sprung above the middle of the action and lit the area. I walked down the cement stairs and made my way toward the lights. It looked as if two guys were going head-to-head with spray cans in front of the two large boards.

Were they really creating graffiti art at a party?

I smiled at the oddity of it, but couldn't help being intrigued. I'd been to a lot of parties where kids just hung around and got drunk off their asses before sneaking off to hook up. But a party where graffiti artists came to paint? Totally out there. Yet . . . totally cool.

The closer I got the louder the hiss of paint and rattling of the cans became.

"Damn, Badalin's work is sick, dude," someone said. "Effin' awesome, man."

Miguel?

I pushed through people to get a better view. One guy was definitely Miguel. He wore all black tonight. Loose jeans, black sweatshirt, and plain ball cap turned backward. His hand held a can, weaving it quickly in the air. Kids rallied around him and the other guy. Miguel was piecing "BADMAN." The letters were with harsh points and slanted lines. Awesome.

The other guy painted "VANCE-one." His style was simpler, with arrows coming out of each side of the word, but his use of color—a variation of blues—was pretty cool, as well.

"Five more minutes!"

These guys were being timed. Miguel didn't look anywhere near being finished. I wanted him to win.

He threw a can down and picked up another to fill in his work. A breeze brought with it a strong whiff of paint. I tried to breathe only through my mouth.

"He'll win."

I glanced over at Petey, who was tugging on one of his bleached spikes. Mateo stood on his other side, with his hands in his front pockets. They were as engrossed as I was. I nodded. I didn't need to ask how he knew. You could just tell by Miguel's level of expertise. His wrist moved in precise movements as he outlined and filled in color, then used black to outline the edges again to make them clean. He knew what he was doing.

He was a graffiti artist and damn proud of it.

At that moment there was no longer any doubt I wanted to learn graffiti art, too. I wanted that confidence, that obvious pride, wanted to create awesome designs with bright colors and bold outlines. The more unique and abstract, the better. My art was like that. I could create and make my own statements without being criticized or worrying my style didn't belong. Graffiti seemed to be the type of art where it paid to be different.

I could be myself through graffiti.

My lips curved. In the cool of the night, surrounded by kids who were into this artistic style, the decision felt right. Like the choice I'd made held important weight.

I couldn't wait to tell Miguel.

Time was being eaten up, and Miguel moved quickly, going through different cans and caps. The watchers were starting to get louder. My gut tightened with the excitement.

"Ten, nine, eight . . ."

The crowd was counting down.

Someone's heavy hand landed on my shoulder and I pivoted around.

"Six, five, four . . ."

Rock. "What?" I asked him, looking back at Miguel.

"It's Beth—"

Time was called. The crowd went wild with shouts and hollers. That guy named Mark was the announcer. He called for quiet.

I turned to Rock. "What about her?"

His eyes were a little big and bloodshot, his wide forehead damp with sweat. He leaned closer. He smelled like weed. "Something's the matter with her. Acting all weird. She said she didn't take anything, but . . ."

My pulse picked up. "Where is she?"

He waved a hand and we took off, jogging back up the hill. Rock's heavy body moved surprisingly fast for his size. The crunch of twigs sounded under his wide steps. I followed him to the side of the house, where lounge chairs were set about.

Beth was lying on top of Derek in one of the lounge chairs. His hands were on her ass. She laughed, her shoulders quivering as if she couldn't stop.

Derek looked at us with a scowl. "Get the hell outta here. We're busy."

I ignored him. Beth's face was pale and she continued to smile all goofy-like.

"Beth, what's wrong with you?"

She looked at me, not saying anything. I wasn't sure if she even saw me. "Beth?" I took a few steps closer, bent down, and snapped my fingers in front of her face.

"I feel . . . so . . . weird." She laughed again.

I gave Derek a hard look. "What the hell did you give her?"

"I didn't give her shit. Somebody gave her punch. I don't know who."

I grabbed a handful of his shirt and pulled hard. *"Don't lie, you freaking perv."*

"I ain't lyin'!" Derek jerked away from my grip.

"For real, Angel," Rock said. "We didn't see. Didn't see who gave it to her."

Taking a breath, I took Beth's arm and tugged. "Sit her up. *Now.*"

Derek pushed her up right and sat beside her.

"Beth, how do you feel?"

"Do you hear . . . my voice . . . sound . . . like that?" Beth stared at me with wide, dazed eyes.

Nerves tickled my stomach. I'd been to enough parties with people high on drugs. "Some asshole dropped her acid."

Acid messed with your head. Left the tripper out of control. I'd never tried acid, never wanted to. I'd heard plenty of stories floating around school about people who tripped, even seen the effects it had caused at a couple of parties. But what I was most worried about was Beth's trip turning into a bad one. I had no idea how much she was given and didn't know how long the effects were supposed to last.

"How long will she be like this?"

"If it's acid, probably hours," Rock said. The smell of sweat mixed with the older scent of weed.

"Rock, get Miguel. We need to get her out of here."

Rock took off.

"Hey, Beth," I said pleasantly, like nothing was wrong. Yeah, right. *Nada*. "This party's kinda weak. So I think we're going to bail. Let's walk to Miguel's ride."

"Riiiiiiide," she said with a short laugh.

"Help me get her to her feet," I told Derek.

Derek hadn't said much in the last couple of minutes. I really had no idea what he was thinking. Only that he was a freaking perv for trying to take advantage of Beth when she was obviously out of it.

"Guys, I can . . . walk," Beth said, as if it were the easiest thing in the world.

And she could, but I still wrapped my right hand around her wrist just in case—hell, I didn't know—she fell or took off for some weird reason. Acid made a person do things she normally wouldn't do.

We rounded the corner to the backyard. There was no side gate. We were going to have to backtrack through the house. I saw Miguel and the rest of the crew walking up the hill. I hadn't been hanging with the guys long, but even in the dark I was already familiar with the way they walked. Miguel was blowing smoke out of his mouth.

Then he stopped.

"What's he doing?" I asked.

"Oh shit," Derek said.

"What?" But then I saw it. A group of guys walking up to Miguel and stopping a few feet away. Miguel threw his cigarette down and lifted his chin once to the lead guy of the group. "Who's that?" I asked.

"Tyler Maya. He's a badass writer with the West Coast Vandals. Miguel and him have a beef going. And Miguel probably burned one of his crew in the standoff."

I didn't know what to do. Beth was staring out into space. Miguel looked ready to throw down. We needed to get out of here now.

Taking a deep breath, I walked toward the crew.

chapter six

CHARACTER
A Figure Used to Add
Something to a Piece
  —Angel's Piecebook Notes
  (I seemed to know a lot of these.)

Towing Beth along, I stopped a couple of feet away from where Miguel was almost face-to-face with the Maya guy. In the time it took to walk over to the guys, they'd already moved closer to each other in the aggressive way guys did when there was only one outcome—a fight.

No way in hell did I want Miguel to get into a brawl and somehow leave Beth and me stranded. If the fight got too out of hand, cops could be called, kids would scatter . . . I'd seen it happen before.

Rock gave me a look as if trying to tell me not to interrupt. The vibe was definitely tense between Maya and Miguel.

"So you think you can take any of my crew?" Maya was saying.

Miguel's head was cocked with straight attitude. "I know, *hombre.*"

Beth let out a giggle, and I tried to "*shhhh*" her, but she was still tripping. Maya's crew looked our way.

"*What, bitch?*" some *chica* standing by Maya asked. "You think this is funny?" She looked Mexican with her pencil-thin eyebrows and beige skin. Her long brown hair was weaved in a whole mess of tiny braids, with colored beads hanging from each end.

Always someone trying to be a badass. "My friend's wasted," I said, looking her up and down. "Leave her alone."

When someone tried to call you out, the key was never to let your intimidation show. Growing up in my neighborhood, kids had to act tough playing ball on the streets or parks. If you showed any fear, then you were usually beat down. But if you showed them you weren't scared, they might just leave you alone. The only exception was, if you knew someone could kick your ass, it was a good idea *not* to play tough. Truthfully, I wasn't intimidated by this *chica.* She was about my height and build. I could likely hold my own if I had to. I'd been in a handful of fights. Never really liked them, but you had to defend yourself when someone swung first. Holding my own wasn't something I had a problem with.

The girl gave me a dirty look. She obviously wasn't used to being stood up to. "Maybe I was talkin' to you."

"Then no, skank, *I* don't think this is funny. Miguel, come on. Let's bail."

A couple of laughs sounded from her friends, with someone saying, "Oooh! She told you, Ronnie. You gonna let her talk to you like that?"

Great. She had her little posse egging her on.

To my amazement Miguel turned to look at me, then Beth, and nodded. "We'll finish this later. We're out."

"Not yet," *chica* with attitude said. She stepped forward, jerked her head at me. "She's new around here. I want to battle her."

My eyebrows furrowed and I smirked. "You want to fight me?"

Maya looked at Miguel. "You accept, Badalin?"

I almost laughed. "Why are you asking *him*?"

"Nah. She's still learning graf. She can't battle tonight."

Learning graf. They were talking about battling with . . . graffiti art? The night just kept getting weirder and weirder. Well, I guess it was better than using knives or Glocks to settle their differences.

"So's Ronnie. If not the chicks, then you and me. Here, now."

Miguel stared at him. It looked like he was actually considering it. I stepped closer to him and leaned into his ear. He smelled of cigarette smoke. "Hey, Beth's messed up. She needs to get out of here. You're our ride. Don't leave us hangin'."

"You gotta run decisions by your *chica*, Badalin?" There was some laughter from Maya's crew.

Miguel's body went rigid beside me. "Fuck you, Maya."

"No, bitch, fuck you."

"Angel?" Something in Beth's voice had me turning around. She wasn't smiling anymore and her arms were crossed. "What's happening?" She looked scared and I felt for her. I just wanted her out of here, away from any possibility of slipping into a bad trip.

"Beth, just keep it cool, okay?"

"Can we go? I just want to go."

"Soon," I said.

"How soon?" Beth's voice had risen. "It's dark here. I don't want to be here anymore."

"Shut that fat bitch up," Braids hissed.

That cut a nerve. "How 'bout I shut you up?"

"You can try."

"All right," I said loud enough for everyone in the two crews to hear. "I'll do it. I'll battle the bitch."

Miguel and the crew looked at me.

Truthfully, I had no freaking idea what I was getting myself into with a graffiti battle. I had zero experience, which wasn't cool, but if this Ronnie with the braids was just learning, too, I might be able to hold my own by creating a piece of artwork that would leave hers in the dust. In fact, I was counting on it.

I wish I could say I was just doing this for Beth's sake, but my decision to explore graffiti had already been made. Since this Ronnie pissed me off, the battle was just taking it a step further, faster.

"When?" Maya asked.

I swung my gaze to Miguel. "Well . . ."

"Give them a few weeks to work on their style. I'll battle you, same time, same place. Two-hour piece."

I'd opened my mouth to say a few weeks wouldn't be enough time, but Mark, the party host, happened to step in the middle.

"We'll have the battle here." He laughed, stroked a hand down his goatee. "I wouldn't miss a battle between Maya and Badalin for nothin'."

My stomach flinched. A battle here? Like Miguel had been doing just a few minutes ago against a member of Maya's crew . . . in front of a whole mess of people?

I just shook my head, kicked my shoe against the ground. I didn't have time to freak out about this now. "Let's just get the hell out of here."

"Hey, Rock," I said to him in the backseat of Miguel's Blazer.

He leaned closer. Beth was between us. The music was loud so I spoke close to his ear.

"Look, thanks for letting me know about Beth tonight. Wouldn't have been cool if she was left alone with . . ." I nodded my head to the front seat where Derek sat.

He pulled back and looked at me. He nodded his head in understanding and gave me a thumbs-up. I smiled.

"If you need any free school passes or forged notes, just let me know."

"Cool."

A few minutes later, Miguel stopped in front of Beth's house.

"Come on, Beth," I said, tugging her out of Miguel's Blazer. I was tired and cold, wishing I was going home to my own couch bed, such as it was.

She fell to her knees on the grass in front of her house, letting out a hysterical laugh. Behind us, Derek snickered. I heard the driver-side door open before Miguel rounded the hood.

"Here." He took Beth's other arm and helped me guide her to her front door. I sat her down on the front step and took a breath.

"Thanks," I said.

"Eh, don't mention it." Under the glow of the porch light, Miguel turned his hat backward on his head. "So you're down, right?"

I knew he was talking about the battle. "Yeah."

One side of his mouth tugged up. "Cool. Got things to do this weekend, but I'll catch up with you Monday."

"All right."

He glanced down at Beth, who stared into space. "Good luck the rest of the night."

I smiled in acknowledgment. I was definitely going to need a lot of luck getting her past her mom's room without making a bunch of noise.

Staring down at Beth, I said, "What are best friends for?"

I answered my own question on that score as I took Beth's key and did my best to quietly unlock the door.

My heart pounded as the hinges creaked in protest. The front room was lit up, but I didn't see her mom. Two empty wineglasses sat on the front room coffee table. The stereo played some low instrumental music.

Beth still sat staring into space and I rolled my eyes. I kneeled down in front of her and took her by the shoulders. "Beth, snap out of it. We need to get you to your room."

She nodded, her eyes wide. I still wasn't sure she got it.

I helped her up and we lost balance, slamming into the side of the house. Beth giggled.

Sighing, I nudged her over the threshold, then followed right behind. I leaned her against the wall and shut the door and turned the lock.

I swallowed. *Nearly there.*

Taking Beth's hand, I started past the living room, halting at the bright article of clothing on the floor. A red blouse.

My eyes widened and I slapped a hand to my mouth. The next item on the floor was a man's tie. I guided Beth through the darkened hallway, trying not to laugh as we stepped over a high heel, and a man's shirt. I paused at her mom's door, where a black bra hung on the door nob.

"That's the sign," Beth said too loud.

"*Quiet.*"

"Means to stay in my room. She has a friend in her bed."

I would have said something dumb, but then I saw that Beth wasn't smiling as she stared at the bra. It hung there, telling Beth not to come in. To stay in her room until morning. I didn't know what to say. To tell her it sucked she had to hide and play invisible as her mother entertained friends in her bedroom. I wondered how often this happened. Why she never told me and why it took me this long to find out. It wasn't the first time I stayed at Beth's, but it was one of the few times I'd been sober.

I nudged Beth along and we made it to her room. I pushed the lock on her door and turned to see Beth already curled on her bed. I helped her pull off her shoes and just left her clothes as she fell asleep on top of her covers.

The pile of blankets I used when I stayed over were on the floor. I made my bed and changed. Before I got under the covers I checked on Beth. She looked pale but seemed to be just passed out. I settled on the floor, then stared at the ceiling until my eyes grew heavy and closed.

It was early afternoon when I returned home. Beth had been seriously hungover when we'd woken late that morning. Her eyes had been bloodshot, her face pale. She'd complained of a headache. Luckily her mom had gone shopping according to a note she left, and the friend that had stayed over was nowhere in sight. I took a shower, got dressed, and told Beth to take it easy before heading for the bus stop. I hadn't bothered to fill her in about the entire night. Only that someone had apparently slipped her some acid and that Derek, like a total perv, had tried to take advantage. Beth didn't seem to want to talk much. I knew I'd have to tell her all about the crew and the battle when she was more herself. I rarely kept much from Beth.

Mom was vacuuming when I came home. Madonna blared from the stereo. Mom seemed to have never left eighties or nineties music behind and was not ashamed of it. She was singing along to "Like a Prayer," moving her jean-clad hips with each push of the vacuum. She and I were about the same build, but she had more hips and bust than me. Most people did.

Mom was only thirty-three, a young seventeen when she had me. That had to have been hard. She'd dropped out of school, took classes to earn her GED. Sometimes I wondered if she missed experiencing the last years of high school like a normal kid. But when she saw me, turned off the vacuum, and continued to sing and dance toward me, how could I forget she still sometimes acted like a big kid anyway? Her fingers snapped as she gave a bad imitation of what she called "the snake" dance where her head sort of tilted then straightened in the air and her body followed suit.

I walked past her, doing my best to ignore her since I was still pissed at her. After dumping my overnight bag on the couch, I turned to go into the kitchen but she caught me with a hand on my shoulder. She was singing into the handle of the feather duster. My lips twitched.

I would not smile.

I would not smile.

Nana walked in from the kitchen, her hand to her chest as she joined in with an off-key Mexican-accented version, and then I didn't just smile, but ended up laughing out loud.

I fell back on the couch. My mother sat with me and I finally joined in for fear she'd never let me be. Luckily the song ended soon after.

"You're a geek," I said to her.

"If I'm a geek, you're a geek by blood." Her lips curved. Today they were the color of sienna. Her eye shadow was pale brown and her eyelashes coated black. Her cheeks were slightly pink from dancing. I'd always known my mom was pretty, but she looked beautiful when she smiled. She got up and turned off the stereo.

"How was it at Beth's?" Mom asked as she started putting the vacuum away.

My stomach let out a low growl. I stood and went into the kitchen. "Fine."

"What did you guys do?" she called out.

"Hung around."

"With boys?"

"Why do you want to know?"

She appeared, leaning against the kitchen walkway. "Were they cute?"

I shrugged, opening a bag of chips.

"Hmm, my *niña* is finally showing an interest in boys. Maybe you'll learn to wear a little more makeup."

Yeah, the reason I wasn't interested in wearing much makeup was because Mom spent so much time using it to impress guys. I bit into a white corn tortilla chip. "What are you talking about? I think guys are cute, and I've known for a while, thanks."

"Yeah, but you're always down on the guys I bring around."

"Have you really looked at the guys you bring around?" I asked with a laugh.

She narrowed her eyes and started toward me. "I know a good-looking *hombre* when I see one, *m'ija*."

I smiled, backing up, finishing off my chip. I knew I'd hit a sore spot. "Yeah, some of them may have been good-looking, but some have definitely fallen into the loser category."

She was finally toe-to-toe with me when she reached out to grab my ponytail. I jumped out of reach and laughed.

"Just wait," she said as she followed me around the kitchen table. "Until you meet Jaíme. He's hot and sweet. A Cancer. They really know how to have a good time."

We stood on either side of the table now and any minute she would make her move for me. "What? Are you going through some weird list of guys whose names start with 'J'? Spare me the details. Please."

I made my move for an escape and spun around to book it out the kitchen doorway. Damn it, Nana was there. I slowed, tried to move back in the direction of the stove, when my mother caught my hair in a fierce grip. The *mujer* always went for my hair! "Ow," I managed with a sharp laugh—half pain, half joking around.

"Some weird list, huh?" She pulled my hair a little more toward the floor and I managed to grab a handful of hers.

"That's what I said," pulling hers harder. Our heads were now sideways, our backs hunched over. The weird thing was we couldn't keep from smiling.

"Let go, Angel." Mom tried to sound stern, but the giggle in her voice gave her away.

"You first."

"Aye, *m'ijas*, both of you are so stubborn. Let go at the same time," Nana said, walking past us.

My eyes were starting to water. *"Mom."*

"All right, but you better let go when I do."

"I will, I will."

She let go, and a second later so did I. We both stood straight and rubbed our tender heads.

"I almost had you," she said with laugh.

"Almost doesn't count."

"I'll get you, my pretty." She sighed, looking at the clock on the wall. "I got to get ready for my shift. I'm going out with Jaíme after work, so I'll be home late." She wiggled her eyebrows. "Don't wait up." She walked out of the kitchen.

My smile faded. She thought she was being funny. But having to deal with her new boyfriends was not fun for me at all. I grabbed more chips and wondered what was worse . . . my mom changing boyfriends every few months or having a mom who just had friends who came over for sex like Beth's? Luckily my mom didn't bring the men into the house unless it was to introduce them to me and Nana and she hardly ever stayed out all night anymore. When I was little I remembered late nights crying for my mom when she wasn't home and having Nana there to rock me back to sleep.

I rolled the bag of chips closed. I didn't know if it was for me, for the past, or for what Beth had to go through with her mom now, but for some reason I wasn't hungry anymore.

On Sunday night, my mom and I walked out of my favorite *taquería*. It was a small hole in the wall compared to the large shopping area with other little shops and classy restaurants. They had the best *carne asada* soft tacos, in my opinion. Mom had just gotten off work and was still in her uniform. She'd swung by the house to get me so we could make a quick run to pick up dinner. I had the warm to-go bag in my hand.

"Angel."

My mom and I both turned toward the voice.

My whole body did a small surprise jerk. Great. Nathan. I stopped myself from touching the messy ponytail I had propped at the top of my head with an elastic band. Seriously, that was the least of my problems since I was used to having my hair a mess. I'd been lazy all day in sweats and a frayed black tee. I probably looked really tired, too. "Hey, Nathan," I said. He had his little sister with him, and it looked like they were coming from the Italian restaurant two doors down. A place I'd never eaten in because my mom said they charged an arm and a leg for a plate of spaghetti.

"Is this your friend, Angel?" my mom asked beside me. She nudged me a little. I refused to look at her to see the teasing smile I knew would be on her face.

"Oh, yeah. This is Nathan from art class and his sister, Yoli."

Nathan offered his hand. This time I did glance at my mom. Her eyes flickered in surprise. Hell, I knew she was impressed. She shook his hand.

"Hi Angel," Yoli said with a shy smile. She'd always liked me since I stuck up for her last summer.

"Don't forget about being on the committee together," Nathan said with a smile.

"Right," I murmured, inside wincing.

"Committee?" My mom looked at me.

Nathan cleared his throat. "The school mural committee."

"Of course," Mom said, covering her ass. I never even bothered to tell her Nathan had asked me to be on the committee. Like she cared, anyway.

A couple walked out of the Italian restaurant. A tall man in a dress shirt and slacks, his black hair neatly styled, a woman beside him with the same matching mahogany hair as Nathan, wearing a pale pink sweater set. Her makeup was understated, almost as if she didn't wear any at all, but somehow you knew she still had some on.

They glanced over at us and I felt my stomach drop. These had to be Nathan's parents.

"*M'ijo*," the man said as he walked over. He looked at me with a frown, then my mother, whose makeup was on so thickly you couldn't help but notice her bright red lips, dark brown eye shadow, and black mascara.

Nathan introduced everyone.

"Angel works with me on the mural committee," Nathan added.

"I see," his dad said in a flat tone. I glanced at Nathan. He met my eyes and shook his head a little as if he wasn't happy with his dad.

"That's nice," his mother said.

An awkward silence followed that was as big as the invisible crater that obviously separated our lives. Nathan's family was perfect, with their expensive haircuts and nicely pressed clothes. My mom and I were rumpled. Our hair was messed up, Mom sort of smelling like onions in her beige waitress uniform with the ketchup stain on her skirt. I knew she had to be uncomfortable when she started stroking my ponytail. She fidgeted when she was nervous.

"Well," Nathan's mother said with a forced smile, "we should be going. It was good to meet you both."

Right. Sure it was. But I just waved to Nathan as my mom and I walked to our 1990 Dodge sedan and Nathan and his family toward their shiny-looking Volvo.

When we were seated in the car, Mom shook her head. "If money makes you all stiff and rigid like that, I don't want it. But Nathan's a nice guy, and cute," she said, sending a smile in my direction.

"He's just a guy I know," I said as we drove off. It figured my mom wouldn't want to know why I hadn't told her about the committee. After all, what did anything that I care about matter?

"It's for the best, anyway. People with money sometimes act like they're better than people without."

I was quiet for a moment before I said, "Kind of like my dad, I guess."

"Kind of." She smiled as she glanced at me. "You don't want to mess with a guy like that."

"Yeah," I murmured. For once I agreed with my mother on something. Too bad I couldn't get my head to agree. Things would be so much easier if I just stopped liking Nathan.

chapter seven

BLOCKBUSTER
Big, Awesome, Square Lettering, Presented
with a Tilt and Often in Two Colors
—Angel's Piecebook Notes
(A technique I'm practicing.)

"Whoa. What happened to your neck?" I shot at Beth on Monday morning when we met at our lockers.

Yeah, I knew what happened. She'd been attacked by a hickey monster who liked to leave suction marks the size of quarters. Two gross purple spots were on the right side of her neck. A smaller one on the left.

Beth laughed, tugging at the hem of her navy blue sweatshirt. An act she only did when she was nervous.

"Derek's what happened. Saturday night."

When I hadn't heard from Beth the rest of the weekend, I figured she was taking it easy after Friday night. We rarely got together on the weekends, but sometimes called to see what was up with each other. Now I knew why she hadn't called. She'd been preoccupied with the perv.

"Tried to rub them off. A lipstick cap, a frozen spoon. They wouldn't budge. And you know how I feel about turtlenecks."

I hated them, too. But still . . . "How'd you guys meet up? What'd your mom say?"

Her smile turned down on the ends. "Derek called me Saturday. His brother dropped him off. We hung out outside."

My eyebrows lifted. "You made out outside? Where?"

She laughed. "We just kissed. No one was around. Then my mom went to bed and I snuck him in my room. Like my mom has any room to talk about hickeys, anyway, with the men she brings home."

I pictured the bra hanging on the door and shoved the image away. "Well," I said, my voice flat, "I told you what he was doing when you were out of it. If you still like him . . ."

"He's okay." She pushed locks of shoulder-length hair closer to her neck. "He tried to do stuff I didn't want to do. Don't know if I'll go out with him again. Not really my type."

I just looked at her. Yeah, real surprising he'd probably

wanted to go all the way with Beth in her bedroom. Why did she go out with him at all? Beth was my best *amiga*, but sometimes I wondered if she even had a type.

Finally I managed to nod in understanding even though I didn't quite understand at all, but nodding seemed like a good idea. Beth had really started messing with the hem of her top. It looked like I was making her feel uncomfortable. Something I didn't want to do.

"So," I said. "How'd he kiss?"

Beth grinned. "Like a snake."

I laughed. *"What?"*

"You know." She stuck out her tongue and wiggled it like a snake might do when it tickles its nose.

I cringed. "Uuuhhhh."

And we both laughed.

I shook my head. "Consider yourself lucky you just got off with some snake bites."

"I used to be a total Big Mac guy, you know," Rock said as he dunked a Mickey D's chicken nugget in sweet and sour sauce. "But once they went all white meat with these babies, I was a goner."

Derek threw a French fry across the table, hitting Rock right in his wide nose.

"What the hell, dude!"

"Save it for someone who cares, man," Derek said.

Miguel and Beth laughed.

"Hey, Rock, I agree with you," I said. Mostly because Derek thought he was a hot shot and Rock was cool in my book. "They're way better now."

He looked at Derek and raised a hand, palm up, as if telling him to stop. *"Heh."*

Derek scowled like a pissed-off little kid who didn't get his way.

I tried to hide my smirk. Really.

The five of us sat in the mall's food court. Miguel had cruised up to me and Beth after fourth period and asked if we wanted a ride to lunch. Like he had to twist our arms. Taking off from school for lunch was always cool.

I'd ordered a cheeseburger—hold the pickles—and a small fry.

"So, Angel," Miguel said, sucking on his straw, "you pick a tag name yet?"

I shook my head and focused on dipping my fry in ketchup. "Not really."

"Why not?"

I nudged up a shoulder. "Still thinking about it." The truth? I didn't know how to go about choosing one.

Miguel nodded once. "Sometimes a name just comes to you and sometimes it takes some thought. Like Rock here is pretty easy, he goes by Roc-one. Derek, Dynamic."

I lifted my eyebrows, but held back. *Dynamic in what? Giving hickeys or snake tongue imitations?* Beth and Derek went on with their business as usual, as if Saturday hadn't happened, as if the polka-dotted evidence wasn't right there between them.

"See," Miguel continued on, "the name can be anything, as long as you want it. You just abbreviate the name into initials."

I'd been wracking my brain, but nothing had really grabbed me. "Maybe . . . Artist."

"I like Artist," Beth added.

Derek snorted. Rock coughed.

Miguel didn't laugh, but looked like he wanted to. "Everybody and their *mamá* chooses that one. You wanna pick something original. Like, unique."

I could feel myself frowning.

"Eh, have you been practicing with the book I gave you?"

"Yeah." I'd spent a lot of the weekend lying around and sketching out designs, even going so far as surfing the Web for info about graffiti at the local library on Saturday afternoon. Obviously I needed to learn more about graffiti since I was going to be in a freaking battle. I learned some interesting facts. Like how graffiti became popular in New York City with a guy who tagged with a name followed by a number that was actually the street number he had lived on, and that graffiti artists called themselves "writers," not the assumed "tagger." A tagger was someone who mainly tagged their name so others were aware of them, not someone who painted pieces. Which I now knew, was short for "masterpiece."

I felt like I was stepping into a whole new world.

"I brought some with, if you want to see . . ." I'd carried my pack in with us, hoping he'd want to check out my attempts at graf designs, but unsure if I was heading in the right direction.

"Let's check 'em out," he said.

Retrieving my new piecebook out of my pack, my stomach danced. I ran a hand over the black hardcover. It was a bound book with about three hundred blank white sheets. I'd made the purchase at my local art store. On the last page, I started writing down notes about graffiti, even definitions of terms so I could start to remember them. "Wipe your hands first," I told Miguel.

He smiled. "Relax, they're clean."

I handed the book to him quickly before I lost my nerve.

Derek sat beside him and smirked at one of my pieces, not saying anything.

"Angel, those are awesome!" Beth, my number one cheerleader. She'd leaned forward to get a good look at the designs. "Will you do my name?"

"Sure," I told her and made myself look at Miguel. I was still waiting for him to say something.

He had the book open to my second attempt. It was just my first name: "ANGEL," with block lettering colored with red and purple fading into each other, and a black shadow behind it with wings coming out of the ends.

"Nice job, Angel."

But it wasn't Miguel's voice.

With the mall crowd, I hadn't heard anyone walking up to the table. My insides squirmed as I raised my gaze and met Nathan's eyes. "Thanks," I said, my voice quiet.

"What do you want, Ramos?" Miguel shifted in his seat, handing over my book, and leaned back with a whole new attitude. Kind of like someone had bumped into him and he was waiting for the person to get down and kiss his black suede Vans.

"None of your business what I want, Badalin," Nathan said.

I swear it was like the volume in the food court dropped a notch. I didn't know about anyone else, but I'd never heard Nathan sound so badass before. And there was that serious look about him again, this time arrowed at Miguel.

Miguel slowly stood up and I got this prickle at the back of my neck.

A sign definite hostility was in the air.

Mierda. What to do?

"I'm making it my business, Ramos," Miguel said.

Too fast, the two took steps toward each other, nearly toe-to-toe.

Miguel smiled coldly. "What are you gonna do about it? You gonna go and run to Daddy like a scared little girl?"

I'd had enough. I shoved my piecebook in my pack and stood up so fast, Beth flinched. That was how tense the atmosphere was.

I joined them, standing close enough to place my hands

on their arms. Miguel was actually quivering slightly with tension and that kicked my nervousness up a notch. Right now I felt obligated to try to break this up. I was the only one on mutual ground, both guys my friends. Obviously nobody else was going to step in.

"Hey, guys," I said. "Let's just chill out a minute."

Neither of them made a move or acknowledged me in any way, just continued to stare at each other. I licked my lips. My stomach was really tight and I had no idea how I could even stop this. If they wanted to fight, it would happen.

From the corner of my eye, I saw a security guard walking in our direction. I wasn't sure if he saw what was going on, or if it would make a difference. "Mall cop," I murmured and stepped away.

At first they didn't move, then finally Miguel stepped back, but not before shoving Nathan in the shoulder hard enough for Nathan to step back. Beth, Derek, and Rock started to move. *Get out fast* was always the best choice when faced with a possible run-in with an adult.

I grabbed my pack and walked over to Nathan. He was still mad-dogging Miguel. "Hey . . . can I catch a ride with you?"

My first thought was to see if everything was all right with him. I knew Miguel had been doing his best to try to piss Nathan off. It wasn't cool.

Everyone gawked at me as if I'd grown an extra head. Or, more like as if I'd lost my head.

"Angel?" Beth called for me. She didn't get it. I wasn't entirely sure I did.

Nathan gave me a nod and a small smile—that made my nerves walk a straight line instead of zig-zagging right and left—which was a total 180 from the disgusted look Miguel was throwing my way. I just looked away, wondering if I'd ticked him off and what he would say to me about it later. I didn't want to create friction with him and blow my chances with the crew, but Miguel was acting like a total jerk. It wouldn't have felt right to leave Nathan alone right now.

Glancing back at Beth, I asked, "You coming, Beth?"

She looked away. "I'll meet up with you later."

Was she staying for Derek or for me—knowing I crushed on Nathan and wanting to give us some privacy? I wasn't about to stick around to find out.

Nathan had done me a favor asking me to be on the committee—even if he'd been motivated by pity—and I had tried to return it by deflecting Miguel's pounding punches on his cute face.

But yeah, I had to admit this wasn't all about returning favors. No matter how much I tried not to, I still liked Nathan as more than a friend.

Nathan had to know any kind of bad behavior at the mall could be reported back to the school and get him thrown off the committee. And I had a feeling that would really bother him.

Looking back toward the table, I had a feeling about Miguel, too.

That provoking Nathan into a fight . . . would have been just fine with Miguel.

"So why'd you do it?" Nathan asked.

We sat in Nathan's truck in the mall parking lot, me fiddling with the frayed hole in the knee of my jeans, Nathan casually slouched in his seat, two fingers tapping on the steering wheel.

I snuck him a quick glance. He stared straight ahead out the windshield. "You mean, why I came with you?"

"That, and why you tried to stop something that could've been bad."

I shrugged out of habit. "Didn't want to see you guys fight."

His tapping stopped as he gripped the steering wheel instead. "So you did it for both of us."

"Not really."

He looked at me. He wasn't smiling.

"You've been my friend longer than Miguel, and you're heading the committee . . ."

"And could have gotten thrown off it, not to mention from track." He shook his head, muttering a curse. "Badalin would have friggin' loved that." He shifted toward me and I thought he was going to go off on a verbal rampage about Miguel, but a small smile curved his lips instead. He reached over and moved locks of hair over my shoulder, his fingertips sliding against my neck. "I guess I owe you."

My gut fluttered, making me look away. I focused on his gray dashboard. "Consider us even. You know, because of the committee."

He nodded, started the truck, shifting his attention out the back window, and reversing out of the parking space. "All right, but you earned your spot."

I looked out the window. How long would he keep lying about the reasoning for my spot on the committee? Or maybe Miguel was making up the whole scenario. I just didn't know.

"Hey, sorry about my dad yesterday." He shook his head. "Sometimes he can be a jerk."

"He was okay," I said. What else could I say? "They seemed like good parents."

"They are. They just have a hard time understanding my decisions sometime."

"I guess parents are supposed to do that."

He smiled. "Probably right."

"So . . . what's with you and Miguel. Why the bad vibes?" I figured now was the only opportunity I was going to have to ask them about their beef.

He paused so long, I thought he wouldn't answer. "Something from a while back."

"Right." I actually wished I knew what this something was. Obviously Nathan didn't care to share.

Radio commercials played into the quiet that stretched between us on the drive back to school.

"Do you like him?" Nathan suddenly wanted to know.

My eyebrows lifted as I stared out the passenger window. I could have played dumb and asked who he was referring to, but I wasn't a total jerk. "He's all right."

"You know what I mean, Angel. You guys got a thing starting?"

I wasn't sure how to answer, since I was caught off guard. Where had this come from? "We're just friends." I'd never discussed with Nathan my tendency to have more guy friends than girls, but figured it was obvious to most people.

"Just friends." He stretched the words out in a way that could have been just a statement or a question. Or maybe wondering if he believed it.

"So . . . where's Misty?" I couldn't help it. I *had* to ask.

"Don't know, probably with her friends."

Were they in the midst of one of those off-again moments?

"I had to order something at the Sports Zone, and I saw you in the food court." He paused, then asked, "Since when have you been so interested in graffiti?"

"Since just recently." I answered hesitantly. Didn't seem like it was his business to know about Friday's party . . . and the whole battle mess. Or maybe I just didn't want to get into it. It was all new and strange to me—why would I think anybody outside of the graffiti lifestyle would understand about battles that were actually art competitions? I hadn't even filled

Beth in on the details. She knew I was into graf and trying it out, but didn't know I was ready to train to participate in a "battle." Sometimes it was hard for me to believe. I'd never been known as a team player. I wasn't used to big families, or large groups of friends. I let people get close to me slowly, cautiously. So to already be considered part of the crew was a big change for me. And I wondered if I could handle it okay.

"I know I've warned you about Badalin, Angel," Nathan said. "And I don't like to sound like some idiot broken record, and this is the last time I'll say it, all right? He's bad news. He brings down the people he hangs with."

I looked over at him. He had a really strong profile and I itched for a pencil and paper to try to sketch him. I shook my head as if to make the urge go away and get back to what we were talking about. I had to admit, I'd always been the type who had to experience something for myself, not go by what other people told me.

"Nathan, you keep telling me Miguel is bad news, but when are you going to back it up?"

He shot me an uncertain glance. "I don't know."

I shifted in my seat and returned to looking out the passenger window. We were close to the school now. "You're my friend, but I'm not willing to break a friendship just because you tell me to." He pulled into the school parking lot and parked.

"Thanks for the ride," I said, unfastening my seat belt and opening the door.

"Wait up." He put a hand on my arm. His skin was warm through my long-sleeve shirt.

I looked at him, his hazel eyes meeting mine.

"I understand what you're saying. I . . . didn't consider it that way. Walk with me to Chun's class?"

I nodded. "All right."

Once we started walking, neither of us mentioned Miguel again. It felt good to get back to joking around with Nathan, smiling as we settled in our seats.

The good sort of vanished when Miguel came into class and set a note on my table before he took his seat. It was a relief Nathan was sharpening his pencil at the time and I didn't have to suffer another *what have I been telling you?* look.

I unfolded the ripped-edged paper and hid it in my lap as I read.

MEET @ THE BATHROOMS—
15 MINS

I glanced at the clock and then over to Miguel. He wasn't looking at me and I didn't know what to think. Or what to expect.

But knew I'd meet with him to find out what he wanted.

While everyone started on a monochromatic still-life project, I stood and headed for the door. After the warning from Nathan, I didn't want Miguel to go first, then Nathan see me go after him, making it look like I didn't care what he thought.

I did care . . . sort of. Nathan was cool, my friend. But I was still curious to know what Miguel wanted. Was it about lunch and my leaving with Nathan? Had I screwed up with the crew?

I walked slowly. If anyone saw me, it was obvious I was totally stalling, wasting time. A popular activity in high school. A minute or so later, I felt my band falling out of my hair. I pulled it off and heard someone walking up behind me. I turned, slipping the elastic on my wrist.

Miguel.

I lifted my chin toward him in acknowledgment, but he didn't return it, just kept walking.

At first I thought he would walk right by me, but he took a hold of my forearm and tugged me along with him, my wooden hall pass dangling in my other hand. I planted my feet and yanked my arm away. "Chill out, Badalin."

He turned and met my eyes. He was ticked. "Let's go. We don't got all day."

"Where?"

"There's something I want to show you. You down or are you goin' back to class like a scared little baby?"

I tossed my hair out of my face. "I told you before, I don't scare easily."

The tension on his face softened and it made my temper settle. "Show me," he said.

He'd laid out a challenge, plain and simple. Fine. "Let's go, then. But make it fast."

He offered his hand again. And this time I took it. His hand was dry, not really soft, but strong. We took off past the bathrooms, straight out the school hallway, and outside toward the portable buildings, the prefabricated classrooms that were built when the schools in Homestead started running out of desk space.

The late-afternoon wind picked up and chilled me, blowing my hair back. I looked all around us, waiting for a teacher or hall monitor to pop out like a boogeyman and catch us, but there were only a couple of kids doing that wasting-time walk through campus.

He led me behind the farthest portable and in between one of the custodial sheds. Finally, he stopped and turned toward me, his gaze pinning mine.

I licked my chilled lips. "Well?"

He still didn't say anything. With my hand still in his, he pulled me closer to him.

My pulse flickered. Our bodies became closer. The moment his chest touched mine, I knew he wanted to kiss me. He lowered his head toward me and stopped with his mouth the slightest inch away. Being this close to him was crazy, crazy hot.

His breath smelled like cinnamon, but I still didn't move into him. He seemed to be waiting for me to move, but I was nervous. Was this a good idea? It was always like this when I was about to kiss a boy for the first time. Exciting and scary all at once.

At times I'd had issues with Miguel's aggressive attitude, at other times, like now, I couldn't deny my attraction to him. I hadn't liked the way he acted at the mall with Nathan. The way he taunted him, doing his best to egg Nathan on. But a part of me knew there was something in their past that I didn't know about. Something that could validate his anger toward Nathan. I just didn't have all the pieces to the puzzle in order to understand who was right or who was wrong.

Maybe he got tired of waiting, because Miguel's free arm went around my shoulders . . .

. . . and he pressed his cool lips to mine.

Right then I wanted to kiss him. Wanted him to want to kiss me.

He released my hand and the other arm circled my waist, pulling me firmly against his chest. He felt harder than I expected. Miguel wasn't a jock, but in some way he worked his chest muscles.

His mouth opened and my stomach tightened when our tongues brushed.

I was kissing Miguel.

He wasn't Miguel Badalin anymore.

Just a guy who saw something in me that interested him. Who didn't see me as one of the boys after all.

chapter eight

TAGGING UP
The Act of Writing Your Cool Signature
with Marker or Paint
　　　–Angel's Piecebook Notes
　　　(My first tag.)

Miguel pulled back.

I blinked up at him, taking in how good he kissed.

He wasn't looking at me, but digging his hand into the front pocket of his loose jeans. "We don't have much time, but I want to show you somethin'."

"I know, we have to get back . . ."

My words trailed off when Miguel pulled out a thick black marker and motioned to the wall of the custodial shed.

For the first time, I noticed beneath a layer of dirt and within scribbles of kids' names were tags in sharp thick letters:

REYES DEL NORTE
BADMAN, DYNMC, ROC-1, RAGER, LOCO-BOY

My mouth opened as I tried to think of something to say, but Miguel was already placing the marker in my right hand, coming up behind me and hooking an arm around my waist. At some point during our kiss, I'd dropped my hall pass on the ground.

"This is the first step as a member of the crew," he said near my ear, "tagging your name with the rest of us."

He secured his hand tightly over mine and guided me to the wall.

"Wait," I said, hovering the pen a millimeter away from the shed.

"There's no waiting, Angel. You said you wanted me to teach you graf. Well, there's a price. Joining our crew by proving yourself. I don't teach outsiders."

I shook my head. "You said I didn't have to tag." I was still trying to make the shift from hot kiss to this. "Why?" This seemed dumb. What was the purpose? Why was I hesitating? It was just a small tag on an old shed where at least fifty other kids had marked their names. Yet this wasn't what I had in mind by joining the crew. This wasn't what I wanted to be about. I wanted to find my place in the art world. Stretch my creative wings with my culture. To be respected for my work. But defacing school property . . .

"Do this, or that's it. You're on your own."

On my own. Hadn't I always been?

But a voice inside me whispered that I could finally find a place in the art world with graffiti. I couldn't deny that tagging, marring public property, went against my beliefs of the beauty of art. And yet . . . I could feel the quick pace of my heartbeat, the excitement I felt with Miguel at my back. With this small test, I would join the crew. Such a small task in order to start becoming a real graffiti writer. To belong. I felt like I stood on the edge of a steep cliff, and down below was Miguel with his arms out saying he'd catch me, but at the same time at my back ready to push me over.

"Come on, Angel," he whispered in my ear. "What's it gonna be?"

I glanced left, then right, trying to see if anyone could see us between the buildings. "I don't know."

"You do know. You know what you want. You want to learn graf. You want to beat that *chica* in the battle. To prove yourself."

"I don't—"

His mouth brushed my ear. "You *do*."

And he was right.

Miguel pushed our hands toward the wall and I let him. The marker hit the surface.

Taking a breath, I dove head first off that cliff.

I wondered if Miguel would be there to catch me, or if I even wanted him to. I'd always been the type of girl who wanted to land on her own two feet.

GRAF ANGEL.

My tag name was Grafangel.

Abbreviated GRAFANGL.

It still made me want to smile. It felt good to have a tag name, to be that much closer to becoming a "writer." The tag had flashed in my mind the second the marker hit the shed. I hadn't hesitated and thought it had to be right. Had to be me.

The bell rang, ending art class. Everyone started shifting, gathering their belongings to take off to next period.

"Angel, I'd like to speak with you," Mr. Chun called out above the rustle of departing students.

I froze with my pack on one shoulder. "Sure," I answered him, avoiding Nathan's gaze, not even daring to glance over at Miguel. I hadn't looked in Nathan's direction since returning to class. But I couldn't ignore him any longer when he rounded my table and touched my shoulder.

I met his eyes, his expression neutral, which was what bothered me most. What happened to the teasing Nathan from the beginning of class?

Deep inside, I knew. Nathan had to have noticed Miguel's and my absence for pretty much twenty minutes of class. Together.

"Don't forget about the committee meeting after school," he told me.

I forced a smile. "I'm there."

He glanced at my shoulders and I realized I hadn't bothered to tie my hair back again. I opened my mouth to say something like, "It's not what you think," but he turned and cruised out the door.

I put my pack on the rest of the way, pulled out my hair from the back, wrapped the elastic band around my hair in a low ponytail, then ambled over to Mr. Chun's desk.

"You wanted to speak to me, Mr. Chun?"

He looked up at me from his grade book. "Angel, I noticed you were gone from class for a while today."

"Oh, yeah, I wasn't feeling that great . . ."

"Miguel Badalin was absent during the same time."

I shifted on my feet. "Really?"

"I don't have to remind you that I give leeway here because I respect my students, but if you abuse the freedom I give, I will take it away."

Embarrassment heated my cheeks. I hated being lectured to, but what I hated most was getting a "talk" from a teacher I respected. I stopped denying anything, stopped speaking period, just tightened my grip on the shoulder straps of my pack.

"You're a good student, Angel. I expect this . . . skipping class from Miguel, but not you. You've been doing well. And you know that to stay on the committee there are academic expectations you must uphold."

I gave a nod that I understood.

"That's all I have to say. I'll see you tomorrow."

"Omigod!"

"*Shhh*. Quiet," I whispered.

Beth covered her mouth, which at the moment was spread wide with a big, ecstatic grin, her eyes twinkling with something like glee. Yeah, glee. Not a word I used often, but that was what sprung to mind.

"He kissed you?" she whispered, strolling with me after school to the courtyard for the first official mural meeting. Beth was coming to hang out for a while. She rolled her eyes. "Omigod." Then she zeroed in on me again. "How was it? Like, totally hot?"

I tried to play it off like it was nothing, but ended up laughing instead. "Yeah."

"Where were his hands? Were your bodies touching?"

I frowned, thinking about it. "Around me. Yeah, our bodies were touching."

"I bet. And to think after you took off at lunch he was *so* pissed."

I stopped her with a hand on her arm. "He was?"

Beth nodded. "Yeah, he was calling Nathan Ramos all kinds of names. Asking me what was up with you. Why you took off. I think he was *jealous*."

"Yeah?" Did Miguel like me that much to be jealous of Nathan? Somehow I couldn't believe it. "What'd you say?"

"What could I say, Angel?" She hooked a curl behind her ear as we continued to walk. "I had no idea why you left, so I just shrugged. I mean, come on, I know you've liked Nathan forever, but doesn't he have a girlfriend? And here's totally hot Miguel Badalin interested in you. *Kissing* you. Don't get me wrong, but has Nathan even given you the time of day?"

"Not really. We're just friends."

"Exactly. Where Miguel here wants to be more." She lifted her eyebrow. "If you know what I'm sayin'."

"I guess." I paused, then asked, "Why did you stay back with them at lunch? Why not come with me and Nathan?"

"I don't know . . . didn't want to be like a third wheel."

"You wouldn't have been."

I really meant it, but she just shrugged. "Besides, Miguel had offered us a ride. With you leaving, I didn't want to bail on him, too."

I didn't bother saying how I felt tied to both friendships with the guys and at that moment Nathan had needed a friend more. I also left out telling Beth about tagging the shed and that I was now an official member of the *Reyes del Norte* crew. Not that Beth was the loyal city activist type against vandalism, but I still felt weird about the little initiation. Yeah, it wasn't that big a deal to write on an old shed. It wasn't like everyone could see the tag, and that there weren't already a hundred names written on the wall from years of previous high schoolers. But I didn't know if I could really put it all in words and explain it to Beth. Or maybe I wasn't sure she'd understand where I was coming from. Or maybe I wasn't so sure myself.

The committee met by the courtyard center wall where the mural would be painted. Beth wandered off to sit and watch. After Nathan assigned duties, the committee finally got around to sketching out sections of the wall with chalk. The area for the mural was bigger than I imagined, at least fifteen feet across, ten feet high. This was going to be one major project. I couldn't stop the anticipation of creating something awesome on this plain stark surface. My fingers actually tingled to get started.

So what if it was a corny school project? I was part of it. Art was inside me, a part of me. Half the time I was so worried about being successful with my work that I forgot how great it made me feel just to *create*.

I realized this as I sketched part of the Viking ship. Nathan was on a step ladder outlining the main Viking, the other kids performing their assigned jobs of sketching out areas of the ship, measuring dimensions, and deciding on colors to use for each part of the mural.

From the corner of my eye, I watched Nathan step down and stare up at his work. I walked over to stand next to him. "Looks good."

His eyebrows were furrowed, his hands powdered with chalk. A light breeze blew his dark hair away from his face. I was interrupting the "zone" he often stepped into while creating.

Just like that he seemed to snap out of it and looked at me with a smile. "Thanks." He checked his watch. "It's time to stop."

"Already?"

"No joke. I hadn't realized the time, either." He called out to everyone to start cleaning up. "Feels good to be doing this, huh?"

"Yeah," I said, smiling. This was where Nathan and I connected. The differences in our lives didn't matter, like how he was a total hot athlete and I wasn't. How he liked blondes with perky breasts, which I *definitely* wasn't. Just that we were artists. Kind of deep, but true.

"What happened earlier with Mr. Chun?" he asked, gathering loose chalk and setting it in his kit.

I started to help him. "Just—you know—seeing why I was gone so long during class."

He nodded.

I held my breath. *Don't ask why I was gone so long.*

"You need a lift home?" he wanted to know instead.

I sighed. "That'd be—"

"She's got a ride, Ramos."

I pivoted to find an attitude-packed Miguel—one shoulder cocked, head tilted back—standing behind me, with the crew sitting over on a bench table with Beth. I'd been so focused earlier on drafting out my section of the mural I hadn't paid attention to what was going on around the courtyard, or really caring, actually.

How long had they been watching me? I skimmed the past hour in my mind, wondering if I'd done anything embarrassing . . .

Nothing I could think of. That was a relief. Too bad the relief wasn't enough to dissolve the guilt I felt itching up my face. Yeah, guilt. Who the sudden emotion was directed at, I couldn't say.

"Cool," I managed to respond to Miguel.

Was the guilt trip because I'd kissed Miguel and had been about to take off with another guy? Or was it because I'd kissed Miguel when Nathan warned me against him?

Or was it choice C: That I liked two different guys and didn't know which one I should keep liking or which to stop?

I concentrated on wiping off colored chalk from my hands on the thighs of my jeans, avoiding Nathan's gaze. He hadn't said anything but I didn't have to be a mind reader to know he probably wasn't happy I was taking off with Miguel. Again.

"Need help taking the supplies back to class?" I asked.

When I finally looked in Nathan's direction, I realized I didn't need an answer.

Nathan was already gone.

Miguel smirked. "Let's go."

I nodded, wondering again what was going on between Miguel and Nathan.

A half hour later, we were all in Miguel's garage, this time with the door closed. Miguel's dad wasn't home, again. I'd asked Petey on the ride over where Miguel's dad was all the time. He'd just shrugged and said, "He works a lot."

I knew Nana was playing bingo at an *amiga's* house tonight, and of course, my mom was working so I didn't bother making it home for dinner. Tonight my dinner consisted of pepperoni pizza from Domino's and Coca-Cola courtesy of Miguel.

And unfortunately a bonus contact high.

"You sure you guys don't want any?" Rock stood in front of me and Beth as he sucked in a serious hit from a joint. He blew out a cloud of smoke straight into our faces. Derek and Mateo were playing Halo 2 on the Xbox and Petey was about to take his hit.

I waved a hand in front of my face and laughed, sitting on the couch with Beth on one side, Miguel on the other. "I'm sure, thanks."

The light was on in the garage, the door closed to the house. No windows were open and I watched the smoke float around us.

Miguel had taken a couple of drags and was now smoking a cig. "Why don't you guys burn it?"

I shrugged, trying not to look at him too much. Our kiss was pretty fresh in my mind. I wanted to act cool like he was—almost like the kiss never happened—but it was still hard to be all casual. "I tried it a couple of times and didn't see what all the hype was about." I looked at Beth.

"Angel's not into it so I haven't smoked in a while."

I lifted my eyebrows. This was the first I'd heard I was basically holding her back. "If you want to, don't let me stop you," I said.

"Really?"

Why did she feel she needed my permission? "Go ahead."

"Maybe you didn't smoke it right or have good enough shit," Miguel suggested to me.

"Could be."

"So why not try again?"

I didn't answer right away. Beth took the joint from Petey, placing it between her thumb and forefinger. She placed her lips around the paper, as if she was going to give it a kiss, and inhaled.

She pulled the joint away—her face looking all scrunched up—and blew out smoke. I thought she might have inhaled too much because she coughed as if she might puke.

"You okay, Beth?" I asked.

She nodded.

My eyes were starting to feel as if something was squeezing them. Funny, how do eyeballs feel tight? Apparently I really *was* experiencing a contact high. I looked at everyone else all smiles and kicking back and wondered why I had to be the outsider here. "I guess I'll try some."

"Cool," Miguel said.

Beth giggled. The bud was already affecting her.

I took the small joint that was now the length of my thumbnail and studied it uncertainly.

Here goes.

*   *   *

Weed made Petey funny.

Or maybe everything was funny when you were high.

"Okay, okay. Check this one out." He pulled most of his bleached spikes down and left up two on each side of his head. "Look, I'm the devil."

"Nah," Mateo said, giggling. Who would have thought Mateo, the quiet one, was a giggler? "More like a two-horned unicorn."

Everyone busted up over that one for some reason.

"You're an idiot, man," Derek let us all know.

I just sat there taking everything in. My mouth was dry but my now warm soda didn't do much to quench my thirst. Beth still sat next to me, her eyelids a little low.

I must not have inhaled good enough before.

I must have also said that out loud because everyone was laughing again, and agreeing with me.

I smiled. I was starting to get to know the crew a little more. Rock was the big easygoing guy. Mateo the quiet one—except when he was high—who kind of just went along with what anyone said. Derek was still the jerk, who liked to put everyone down. And Petey could be quiet, but when he was high he liked the attention. Miguel was the leader. The crew seemed to look up to him, but still acted at ease with him.

"What time is it? I gotta get home." *Homework, homework.*

"All right," Miguel just said.

"Hey, Angel?" Petey the chatterbox asked. "So how's it feel to be the first and only *chica* to join *Reyes del Norte*?"

"Feels cool."

"A girl of many words."

I just laughed. That's all I could do at the moment. Crazy.

"You're in the crew?"

I turned to Beth. Crap, I still hadn't mentioned it to her. "Yeah. I'll tell you about it later." I would have to explain to her how I was still adjusting to the idea, not that I was intentionally keeping it from her.

She smiled. "Okay."

I looked over at Miguel, his body slouched and totally relaxed. His fingers were playing with his wallet chain again, sliding the links between his forefinger and thumb. A spray can sat on a shelf above our heads. I'd always been fascinated by what could be created with a simple object such as a pencil or a paintbrush. Now I was delving into what could be created with a can of spray paint. Something that wasn't so easily controlled.

"Why, Miguel?" I murmured. "Why graffiti?"

He looked at me and one side of his mouth curved up. Smoke floated around him. His eyes looked red-rimmed. "It's the ultimate freedom of artistic expression. Nobody to answer to. Just you, your vision, and your paint. Did you know there are graf artists that make it their life traveling the world just to piece with artists in different countries? They just hop a plane, and take off. Not knowing where they're going, where they'll be tomorrow." He leaned forward, his eyes a little clearer. "You want that feeling of freedom, right? You're tired of the school putting you down for adding our culture to your art. You're tired of the guys like Grayson saying you messed up your chances because you put who you are in your project instead of being like everybody else. Man, that's so much shit. We have to be who we are inside through our art. We need to *be* somebody." He leaned back, smiling. "Expressing yourself through graf is the best feeling in the freaking world. You'll see."

And I hoped I would.

Maybe that was the appeal to me. Someone was telling me how great and open-minded graffiti was and I wanted to experience that feeling myself.

I needed to feel it.

Miguel drove with everyone slapped up against one another in the Blazer like markers packed in a box. After dropping off Beth, we arrived at my house. Miguel told me he'd catch me tomorrow.

Yeah, *catch me tomorrow.* As in no smile good-bye, no call tonight, no little glance that told me he remembered our kiss. Didn't quite know how I felt about that. Maybe the kiss at school didn't mean anything. We hadn't gone out on a date or anything. He hadn't even asked what had happened with Mr. Chun like Nathan had, now that I thought about it. But funny thing, it was easier not to worry about it than I thought . . .

An hour later, I was so freaking tired. My eyes were lazy,

body like dead weight. I wanted to go to sleep, but I had more homework to finish. I didn't like the after-pot tired feeling. Nothing was funny anymore, especially now that I was alone. I had TRL blaring on TV like my own personal concert, trying to keep myself awake.

The phone rang and I grabbed the remote from the arm of the couch, lowering the volume, before answering the cordless. "Hello?"

"Hey, Angel, it's Nathan."

I blinked. "Hi."

He cleared his throat. "Can you talk?"

Was he kidding? "Sure."

"So . . . what are you doing?"

I looked down at my homework sitting on my lap, and almost lied, but with Nathan I didn't have to act like I wasn't doing my work because it wasn't cool. He knew what I had to do to stay on the committee. And I definitely wasn't going to mention I was coming down off a marijuana high. Didn't even want to go there.

"Just finished my English lit assignment. What about you?"

He told me he'd just hacked away at his school work, too, and we went on to talk about the mural, about school. Everything seemed natural. Like we were good friends passing time even after our awkward moment earlier. It was great that we could fall back into a friendly rhythm.

He started in about his weekend job. "I didn't know you worked weekends? Where?" I asked.

"Three days. Friday through Sunday. I work for the city rec center with the Little League sports. You know, like refereeing."

"Cool."

"The games are at Coolridge Park on Fridays around five-thirty. It's funny watching the little guys run around. You should come."

"Maybe I will."

We were quiet for a moment, but I didn't feel nervous like I *had* to fill the silence.

"I like talking to you," Nathan murmured in my ear. "It's nice."

I felt a little warm with his words in my ear and the quiet of the house. "I like to talk to you, too."

"Maybe we could go grab something to eat sometime."

I stilled. "That would be cool."

"Some night after a mural meeting, well, when I don't have track." He let out a small laugh. "You know."

"Sure." Yeah, I knew. I also knew when people didn't set exact dates, they usually forgot. Still, it was cool of him to ask. "So, ah, how's Misty these days?"

He cleared his throat. "She's good. Things are different since we called it quits a couple of months ago. We've been together too long not to remain friends, though."

Was it bad to feel good about this news? "All right," I said. "Well, I better let you go."

"Angel?"

"Yeah?"

"I'd like to call you again."

"Okay. See you tomorrow." I pushed the disconnect button on the phone.

I stared up at the ceiling and I could feel a smile forming on my face.

Slowly my good vibe faded, as I ran a finger across my bottom lip and picked at a spot of dry skin. I was forgetting one big fact.

That I'd kissed Miguel today at school. That I was a member of the crew because graf was a medium of art I wanted to explore. The problem was, I liked both boys for different reasons. They were two independent guys, and I admired them both for their unique talents.

Nathan was awesome with his realism. He created classic beauty out of anything he set his mind to. His confidence poured onto his canvas, and it was weird, but sometimes it almost made me weak in the knees how beautiful his creations were. I'd never admit out loud how much I wished I had even a small amount of his skill.

Miguel's art was rough, strong, and shouted to the world that he was his own person. His work made bold, brilliant statements. I had to admit it was more my style, a place of creativity where I could belong and I wondered if I really wanted to throw going out with him into the mix. Any relationship that was more than friends could get messy, changing more between us than I was ready for. I could find myself wrapped up in something I didn't want, just like how I was suddenly in the middle of a graffiti battle.

I shut my eyes. Maybe I should change my tag name.

To Confused Angel.

"Angel, wake up. Damn it, you better wake up *now*."

I pulled the blanket over my head. The light was killing me. Didn't know what time it was. Didn't care.

My mom ripped the comforter off my head. I squinted against the glare. She stood over me next to the pull-out bed. Her lips were in a straight line and her eyes focused on me. Big time. She was pissed about something.

"What?"

"How long have you been smoking pot?"

My insides jerked but I managed to turn over on my stomach, avoiding her gaze. "Don't know. What. You're talkin' about."

"You think I'm an idiot, Angel?" She stuffed the shirt I'd worn that day right in my face.

"What the hell!" I grabbed hold of it and threw it. The top landed on the floor.

"Did you think I wouldn't smell your reeking clothes even though you buried them deep in the hamper? I walked into my room and I could smell that crap right away."

I'd remembered to take a quick shower, scrubbing and washing out the smoke from my skin and hair. Should have done a load of laundry, too.

"Answer me. How long have you been smoking?"

I was caught. I knew it. Denying only worked so far with my mom. "It was one time," I muttered into my pillow.

"The last time. Do you understand me, Angel? Or I mean it, you will regret it the rest of your high school days!"

My hands fisted under my blankets. "All right, already. The last time! Can I go back to sleep now?"

Why was it she was only on my case when I did something wrong?

She turned abruptly, her hair swaying with the movement. I stuffed my face into my pillow and watched the colorful shapes form behind my closed eyelids until I calmed down. Until my body relaxed and I fell asleep.

chapter nine

SCRUB
An Outline
Filled in Fast with Sprayed Lines
     –Angel's Piecebook Notes
     (The first technique Miguel teaches me.)

"**h**old the can like this, and move your wrist quick-like."
Miguel's hand covered mine over a spray can, holding it at an
angle. His chest was close to my back.

It had been an unusually warm Tuesday for the end of
September, with no wind passing through Miguel's square,
compact, fenced backyard. The sun seemed to be aimed
right on his house. Miguel let go of me and stepped away. I
pressed the nozzle, but I guess I wasn't moving my hand

fast enough because too much paint was forming in one spot.

"That's wack," Derek yelled out from behind me. The perv was dissing me. Big surprise.

"Lay off, Jack," I shot back. What the hell did Beth see in him?

"It's good for a first try," Petey said from my right.

"Yeah, her first try," Mateo joined in from the left.

I smiled at Petey and Mateo—*they* were always cool to me—before glancing over my shoulder. Beth sat beside Derek under a tree, watching the paint lesson. They weren't cuddling or anything, but I had a feeling they would go out again if one of them felt the urge.

I turned toward them, cocking my hip to the right. "Why don't you get off your ass and show me better?" I taunted him.

Derek just sneered and shook his thick head. I was beginning to wonder if Derek had any artistic drive at all. I hadn't seen much of his work, and while the crew practiced, he just sat around, like he was doing now.

"Here," Miguel said, shaking a can of black paint, making that little ball-in-the-can rattle. "Watch."

And the expert that he was, he threw up "BADMAN" in block letters on the plywood, ditched that can for another, and began to fill in the outline with thick blue lines in steady back-and-forth movements.

Damn, he was talented. "I'll never be able to do that," I told him.

"Not without practice."

True. But my mom wasn't even supportive of my regular artwork, let alone allowing me to set up my own backyard graffiti studio.

He grabbed the black paint, outlining the letters again. Added some touch-ups, but it was already a masterpiece in my book.

"Just try practicing your tag for now till you get the hang of the can," he told me. "Don't be intimidated. It's just paint, something you've probably been working with for years."

I sighed. Never with a spray can before. I knew three weeks wasn't going to be enough time to get ready for the battle. I continued to practice, giving my letters hard points and long lines. I used a "skinny" cap for the tag. Turns out you never wanted to use the tips—caps—that came with the cans. There were all kinds of different tips with varying widths of sprays—fat and skinny ones with special names. Fats were for fill-ins, and skinny tips usually for the outlines, unless you used a fat cap for a tag and attempted to "flare" the ends of your letters. I'd seen some pretty awesome pics of flares by pro artists. It was going to take so long before I ever reached that level. I'd only started to see a small difference with my writing, but my finger throbbed from pressing the cap for almost an hour and I needed a rest.

"I'm done for today." I turned around. Everyone had disappeared. Beth and Derek had gone to the garage hangout. The other guys had gone home.

I threw the can in a bucket and flexed my hand. I had smears of black paint on my fingers and black under my nails.

"Cool," Miguel said and swung his arm around my shoulder like he'd done the first time he'd brought me to his home. It didn't bother me so much now that we'd swapped spit.

He looked down at my Oscar the Grouch T-shirt. "Why don't you wear tops that fit tighter?"

I frowned, glancing down at my loose top. "What for?"

"*Chicas* look hot in those little tops."

I rolled my eyes. "Hello, *Jack*. I'm not like other girls."

"No kidding." I couldn't tell what he meant by his bland tone, but I forgot about whatever it was when his face scrunched and he asked, "What's with calling me 'Jack'?"

"Like a joke." Yeah, my words were edged with sarcasm.

He just stared at me with no expression. "Don't make me laugh."

"Whatever." What was his problem today?

Miguel brought his hand around the back of my neck, pulling me toward him.

I tensed, putting a hand to his chest to stop him. "Miguel . . ."

He dipped his head and brushed my lips. "What?"

I glanced down at my hand against the dark gray of his T-shirt. "Look, I was thinking . . ."

He lifted my chin, and kissed me again. "Say it."

But he wasn't giving me a chance. I stepped back far enough for his hand to fall to his sides. "We should just be friends." This decision finally became crystal clear. I wasn't as comfortable with Miguel as I should be to keep making out with him. Nathan changed things for me.

One side of his mouth curved up. "We are just friends. The kind that go out sometimes."

Shaking my head, I said, "That's not cool with me."

"So what? You want a boyfriend?" He said "boyfriend" like that was so not an option.

"I don't want that, either."

His eyes narrowed and the small smile fell away. "Why?"

Again, I zeroed in on the truth. Nathan. But I so couldn't tell Miguel I was crushing on another guy. Not with this "thing" they had going on between them, and besides, it just wasn't cool to tell someone that.

"Because I don't want the guys treating me different if we go out." And that was part of the truth.

"What do you care what they think?"

I crossed my arms. "I care what my friends think. I care about being respected."

"So now the guys are *your* friends." He made a snort sound. He stood a couple feet away from me and I could tell my turning him down really bothered him. His eyebrows were lowered over his eyes and his shoulders looked rigid and stiff.

"You're saying they aren't?"

He took a quick aggressive step toward me that nearly made me retreat. "Just remember something. You're only part of *Reyes del Norte* because of *me*. If I say you're out, you're out, and nobody would give a shit."

Licking my dry lips, I jerked a shoulder like it didn't bother me, even though I knew his words were true, and I *did* care. The idea of people being around me because Miguel told them to was ignorant. Maybe Rock, Mateo, and Petey did only act like I was their friend because of Miguel.

"Whatever, then." This conversation was over. With not much to more to say, I asked, "Can we just take off now?" At the moment, Miguel was only interested in kicking an empty spray can around the small patch of lawn.

The can slammed into his fence. "What 'we'?" He stopped and looked at me with a serious scowl.

I scowled right back. He knew damn well he'd offered me and Beth a ride home. But I never asked twice. "Forget it. We'll walk."

He raised an arm toward the house. "Go. No one's stoppin' you."

"Right." My face heated, and not from the sun. Somehow Miguel managed to make me feel like crap for *his* pissed-off attitude.

I stomped over to the side garage door and slammed it open.

Beth and Derek both jerked up from the couch, Beth shoving her shirt down over her chest. Derek let out a curse as I whirled away from them.

I didn't think my face could feel any hotter, but it did. "Sorry," I muttered over my shoulder. "I'm out of here."

"I'm coming with you," Beth called out. She followed me as I walked out of the garage through the side gate of the backyard, just wanting this day to end.

I jerked open Miguel's Blazer door parked in his driveway and yanked out our backpacks and my sweatshirt. A cool breeze was blowing just fine in front of Miguel's house, cooling my face.

"What happened?" Beth asked, as I slipped on my pullover. "Why are we walking?"

Inside I was feeling like an idiot with weird emotions clawing inside me. Anger for Miguel not treating me like a real member of the crew, just like some girl he felt he could go out with anytime he wanted. Guilt for shooting down his kiss and embarrassment for walking in on Beth. So I just blurted out the straight truth, taking off for the nearest bus stop. "I wouldn't kiss Miguel and he got bitchy."

"Why wouldn't you kiss him?"

"Because I didn't want to, Beth. All right?"

"Slow down," Beth said, huffing a little beside me.

So I did. I didn't realize I was going so fast. I was just so pissed off.

"Why didn't you want to? You said earlier kissing him was hot. Is it because of Nathan? I thought we agreed—"

I halted and spun toward her. "*We* don't decide who *I* like, all right, Beth?"

Two bright spots formed on my cheeks. "What-ever, Angel."

More guilt tried to worm a way inside my head, but I let my anger duke it out with the other feelings, and guess what? Anger kicked ass.

"And look who's talking, anyway, I thought you didn't want to go out with Derek again?"

Her eyes skittered away. "It just . . . happened."

Yeah, she just *happened* to trip, fall on her back, and—lo and behold—her top flips up with Derek right there to land on top of her. I just shook my head. No more was said as we parted ways at the main street, Beth walking home in one direction and me walking toward the other.

"Hey," I said into the phone that night.

"Hi," Beth said.

I blew out a breath. "Look, I shouldn't have taken my attitude out on you earlier. It wasn't cool." I'd been feeling guilty ever since I cooled down. I would never have yelled at her if I wasn't all twisted over my argument with Miguel. Beth and I had never even been upset with each other before. I'd felt so weird over how we left things, I had to call her and set it right between us again.

"I shouldn't have been pushing you about Miguel or Nathan, either," she told me. "Totally your life, not mine."

I picked up a pencil and started doodling circles on the open notebook on my lap. One small circle that I went over and over until I thought it was just right, then a slightly bigger one around the smaller one. "It's just, I don't know, I think I like Nathan a lot. Miguel, I'm not so sure." I gave a disgusted look even though she couldn't see me. "He acted all dumb today, almost like a totally different person."

"Derek said sometimes Miguel gets in these moods. It's too bad about his mom."

"Whose mom?"

"Miguel's. I guess she died a couple of years ago in some kind of robbery. Innocent bystander. Isn't that crazy?"

"Damn," I whispered.

We were silent after that, as we tried to imagine our moms being taken away from us like that.

"Well," I finally said. "I just wanted to say that I'm sorry I acted like a bitch."

She laughed a little. "Me, too."

I smiled. Things would be okay with Beth. I wasn't so sure how things would be with Miguel, but we'd see. "All right, then." I thought about asking about Derek, but I didn't want her to feel uncomfortable so soon after we made up. "See you tomorrow."

"Yeah, later."

I clicked off the phone and set my notebook aside—I could only handle concentrating on homework for so long—and dug out my piecebook from by pack. I had also tried my hand at stickers. I'd picked up a pack of full-page-size labels and drew a couple of "GRAF ANGEL" designs on them in purple and black, then had cut them out and stuck one on the front of my black notebook cover and the others on blank pages. A third of my book was already filled up, and not just with my own drawings. I'd asked Petey and Rock to design a page each. There was also a page where each of the crew had tagged in it, yeah, even Derek since he was part of RDN. It was a small pleasure knowing his tag sucked.

I opened the book to a fresh page, grabbed a pencil, and started sketching. Hours passed, then my eyes began to droop and I stood to get ready for bed. I had a passing thought that I didn't finish all my homework before I crashed for the night.

Mr. Chun had allowed us class time on Wednesday to brainstorm for the mural committee. The committee members were in the courtyard, sitting at a picnic table during fifth period talking about the committee schedule. How exciting.

"And we also got the list of the locations where the winning school will be creating the murals through town," Nathan said.

I finally snapped to attention at this. "Can I see it?" I asked the same time as Lydia.

Nathan smiled. "Here, Lydia, you're closer to me. Just give it to Angel when you're done."

Right. She was only, like, maybe a foot closer. Big deal.

"So does everyone think two days a week is enough to finish the mural by January? Should we add another day?"

"No thanks," muttered a kid named Billy. "Some of us have lives."

A couple of the committee members laughed.

I murmured in agreement that two days was good, trying to wait patiently for Lydia to *hurry her ass up*. When she started to copy down the list in her notebook, I couldn't hold my impatience. "Hey, Lydia, let me have a quick look before you start copying the list."

"I'm not going to copy the whole thing, just a few locations near my house."

"Well, I'm not going to copy anything down, just take a quick look."

Her eyes rolled behind her glasses. "If you could just wait a couple of minutes."

"If *you* could wait like *one* minute."

"Ladies," Nathan cut in. He casually offered his hand to Lydia. "Why don't I just make it easier and make a copy for you and anyone else, okay, Lydia?"

Lydia's lips twisted but she finally handed it over to Nathan. "Fine."

"Thanks," he said and handed the paper to me. "Here, Angel."

I grabbed it, merely nodding my thanks, and scanned the list. Some parks I didn't recognize, a few historical sites in the old town I did know. Lower and lower and I went down the list . . .

Until the very end.

No.

I started from the top again, slowly this time, using my finger as a guide to make sure I hadn't accidentally skipped over it.

I let my hand fall to my lap and just sat there.

"Angel, what's up?" Nathan asked.

I shook my head and handed back the paper. "Nothing."

He looked at me like he knew I was lying, but he continued talking to the group. "All right, we'll keep the schedule. Class is about to end so I'll see everyone after school." He smiled. "With copies."

Everyone started walking away and Nathan put a hand on my arm. "What's up with you?"

I stood. "I didn't see North Caesar Park on the list."

He frowned. "Never heard of it."

Yeah, you *wouldn't have.* "Why do you think it's not on the list?"

He scooped up his binder and pencil. "Couldn't tell you. Is that a problem?"

I forced a shrug. "No big deal."

The bell rang.

His eyes met mine. "You sure?"

"Yeah."

"Hey, Ramos!" a jock, named Andrew Harper, called out.

Nathan nodded his head to him. "Hold up!" He looked at me. "See you after school, then." He waited until I nodded and then took off, jogging toward his friend.

I stood there for a minute and turned toward our work-in-progress. The mural was just an outline at the moment. No color, no depth. Empty. Sort of how I felt now, knowing that not only was my park not being upgraded but it couldn't even warrant a frigging mural.

I stewed over this all through sixth period. Afterward, when Beth and I were at our lockers, Miguel and Derek came by. Beth and I hadn't gone with them to lunch. I'd decided avoidance was the best course after Miguel's little temper tantrum yesterday.

He nodded his head at me. "What's up? You coming over?"

I lifted my eyebrows. I could play this two ways. Stay pissed at him for being a complete jerk yesterday, or be like him and act like it didn't happen.

"I don't know. Got a mural meeting."

His lip curled. "You don't got to go to each one."

"True."

"Let's go, then. Before you know it, the battle will be here and you're not gonna know shit."

He was right. I needed a lot more graf practice. Even though I was creating small "throw ups" I didn't feel that comfortable handling a spray can yet. But, truthfully, Miguel didn't have to do much convincing. Ever since finding out North Caesar wasn't going to be part of the community mural project, I sort of felt like I was in a weird place. For the past three weeks, I'd done nothing but breathe my mural presentation. It had given me a purpose with my art, given me a focus. When I'd lost the competition, I had fallen to a low point until Nathan had given me a spot on the committee. Something to work toward. Now, here I was back to not knowing what to do. Floating.

Yeah, I had agreed to learn graf and compete in a battle . . . but I guess I hadn't made a real personal decision to put all my energy into learning and doing my best to win.

Until now.

"All right," I said. "Let's go practice."

chapter ten

BOMB
To Tag an Area with All Kinds
of Signature Throw-ups
　　　　–Angel's Piecebook Notes
　　　　(Sometimes I bomb with the choices I make.)

"What happened Wednesday?"

I wouldn't meet Nathan's eyes across our two art tables. It was now Friday. I'd ended up playing sick all day Thursday. Who knows if my mom bought it, but she let me stay home. I wasn't proud of it, but my feelings about the committee had changed and the only way I could deal with things was not to deal with them at all. To avoid them. I'd been doing this with Nathan, too. But even I knew I couldn't avoid things forever.

"I guess I was kind a tired," I answered after a noticeable pause. "Not feeling well."

"That's why you missed yesterday," he said.

Leaning back in my chair, I finally looked at him. "Yeah. I'll let you know the next time I can't make a meeting."

His head tilted slightly, his eyes narrowing. "How many you plan on missing?"

I hesitated. Nathan was rarely so blunt with me. "I don't plan on missing any more, but sometimes things come up. I'm not going to be the only one to miss a meeting." My last sentence was said defensively.

"I guess you're right," he said in a tone that said he didn't really believe it. Then as was his habit in the beginning of class, he got up to sharpen his pencil.

Sighing, I felt that little clutch in my gut—guilt. Nathan hadn't needed to nominate me to be on the committee. I knew I wasn't bringing anything extra special to the mural that any other kid in advanced art couldn't bring. But he had still given me a spot. Here I was letting him down by not following through with my commitments. And for what? Because my park was neglected by the city again? Because I didn't know how to tell him it bothered me?

Yeah, I knew it wasn't Nathan's fault my park was omitted from the project but I'd been letting him take the blame, even though it didn't really make any sense. I may not feel as passionately about the committee as I once had, but I should still do my best to give the committee my attention. For the sake of my friendship with Nathan, if nothing else.

When he sat back down, I said, "It won't happen again if I can help it. All right?"

He nodded. "All right." He didn't sound convinced.

And him not believing me bothered me more than it should. I dedided to do something about it.

After last period, I stood with Beth at our lockers. "So we can take the bus to the park and just hang out and watch the game for a while," I was telling Beth. I tried to tell myself the only reason I wanted to watch Nathan ref a game was to make sure things were still cool between us. "I mean, what else is there to do, you know?"

"Sounds good," she said. Then, "Are you sure you don't want to go by yourself?"

I looked at her, surprised. "Why? You have other plans?"

"Not really. Just, you know, the third wheel thing."

I knew her mom made her feel like a third wheel at home, but I didn't think I ever had. "Nathan doesn't even know I'm coming." In fact, I kind of needed Beth to come as support in case Nathan didn't want to see me. "But if you don't want to go . . ."

Miguel and Rock strolled up to us, interrupting our conversation. Nodding once at us, Miguel said, "Let's roll."

Beth started messing with the books in her locker.

I scraped at my bottom lip with my teeth. Great, what should I say? "Got to get home today, actually."

Tilting his head to the side, Miguel jerked a shoulder. "I'll give you a ride home this time."

Gee, how generous of him.

Miguel had been giving me rides to his house from school, but still not rides *home* because, well, I'd stopped asking after he'd backed out once with his earlier temper tantrum when I wouldn't make out with him. I'd learned my lesson there.

I zipped up my pack. "Sorry. Can't today."

He didn't comment.

I shoved my ponytail over my shoulder and looked at him.

He frowned at me, then moved his attention to Beth. "You coming, Beth?"

I slid a surprised look at Beth. Not because I didn't know what she'd answer—I knew she was coming with me—but because I was shocked that Miguel had asked her along. Derek wasn't even with them.

Beth beamed a smile—hesitated for a *half a second*—and nodded. "Yeah, sure."

I blinked.

She glanced at me, then away. "We'll get together later, okay, Angel?" She slammed her locker closed. "Call me tonight."

I finally found my voice. "All right."

"Later, Angel," Rock said.

"Yeah, later."

Miguel gave that half smirk before they walked off down the hallway toward the parking lot.

Beth threw her head back and laughed at something Miguel must have said. I looked around the hallway.

I was all alone and hadn't realized it until now.

I'd decided to not go to the park at least five times before I finally hopped a public transit bus to the other side of town. It was almost like being around Nathan was top priority and that didn't sit so well with me. But I didn't want to sit at home on a Friday night since I already told Miguel I was too busy to hang out with the crew. The battle was getting closer every day and here I was not even ready. Every time I thought about the competition, I could feel my pulse pick up, my gut tighten. All I saw was me with the can, my paint dripping on the board and everyone laughing and shouting things at me.

Toy.

You're so wack.

You suck.

Great.

The game had already begun when I walked across the park to the baseball diamond. The wind was blowing pretty good and my hands were stuffed in the front pocket of my black hoodie. Adults and kids, probably families of the players, sat on both bleachers on each side of the ball field. I saw Nathan standing behind home base, with a little kid kneeling beside him in the catcher position. Another kid about six or seven was standing beside home plate, trying to hit the ball an adult pitched to him.

The first few bleachers behind Nathan were clear of people, so I took a seat. Even though it was chilly, he wore a white T-shirt and faded jeans. One hand was tucked inside the front pocket as he leaned his weight on his left foot. Some kind of blue plastic handle stuck out of his back pocket.

The batter smacked the ball and took off for first base. Nathan turned to toss the catcher a ball, and he caught sight of me. A slow smile formed on his mouth, like he was glad to see me. I smiled back, relieved. I hadn't known what his reaction would be when he saw me. The little catcher threw erratic pitches to the adult pitcher. It was kind of funny. Nathan took the handle out of his pocket, which ended up being a small broom, and brushed off home plate, then the next batter skipped to the plate.

I watched the game and Nathan for the next half hour. Watched how at ease he was with the kids. He'd stop and help a kid hold the bat correctly or tell a kid "good hit" when he or she came running home. This helping young kids was a side to Nathan I hadn't seen before, but then I'd never seen him around any younger kids other than his little sister. Obviously, I hadn't seen Miguel in a situation like this and could never even picture him helping others.

When the teams lined up and all high-fived one another after the game, I rose from the bleacher. I felt a flutter in my stomach as I went up to the fenced backstop. Nathan smiled at me as he walked up to the other side of the fence.

"It's cool you came," he said.

I nodded. "You were right. It was fun to watch." Even more fun to watch Nathan. The wind had hair flying in my face even though my hair was in a ponytail. "Kinda windy."

"Yeah. Hey, what are you doing now? How'd you get here?"

I was embarrassed to admit I went out of my way to take the public transpo across town, but how could I lie? "Bus."

"I'll give you a ride home . . . unless you're hungry. I haven't had anything since lunch."

I shrugged even though my pulse sped up. "Could eat."

"All right. Just give me a few minutes to clean up here."

Five minutes passed as he collected baseball equipment and shook hands with the coaches. He rounded the backstop and waved me over to walk to his truck. It was a relief to be inside the warmth of the truck, instead of against the cold wind.

Nathan's hair was blown back away from his face. My hair probably looked a mess, too. I pulled my band out of my hair and shook it out.

"Your hair is so long."

I rolled my eyes at him. He wasn't really smiling, but his expression looked relaxed. "I know. It's just easier to tie it back."

He grinned. "I meant that as a compliment. It looks nice down."

My cheeks warmed. "Thanks." But I still gathered my hair with my hand and tied it back again.

He started the truck. "What do you feel like eating?"

A list of fast-food restaurants ran through my head. "Whatever you feel like."

"You're going to eat, right? Not order a salad and pick at it?"

"Ah, yeah. I kind of need food to, like, survive."

He laughed and drove off.

A few minutes later Nathan pulled into Applebee's, a popular restaurant hangout for the younger crowd. There weren't exactly a lot of restaurant choices in small-town Homestead. For some reason my stomach began to tingle with nerves. This wasn't a date. I knew that. I even repeated it to myself when he put his hand at the small of my back as we walked to our table.

A freckle-faced waitress took our order—cheeseburger for him, nachos for me—while some kids chattered and colored on menus beside us. Our talk fell to the mural, of course, as he updated me on the progress of the last meeting, and about the competition we were up against. I didn't ask him why he wanted to be part of the committee. Mostly because I wasn't ready to share why I had wanted to be a part of it.

After we ordered and I was stuffed with nachos, I grinned. "I told you I could eat."

He laughed. "You did, huh? I thought you were going to bite my fingers for stealing a chip."

"Yeah right, *Jack.*" I tossed my balled-up paper napkin, hitting him square in the chest. We laughed.

He wiped his mouth with a napkin. "Before I forget I picked this up for you." He took a folded paper from his back pocket and opened it. I'd seen him lift it from his dash and stuff it in his back pocket before we'd left his truck. He handed it to me. "Thought you might be interested."

"All right." Skimming the information, I read a few details.

. . . ILLUSTRATOR CONTEST . . . UNDER 18 . . .
ONE SEMESTER FREE ILLUSTRATOR COURSE . . .
INSTRUCTOR JOSH BLAKE . . .

It took me a moment to take in the implications. "Why . . . would you give me this?"

"Why not?" His expression bordered on surprised. "A semester of free instruction at the junior college by a top illustrator? That's an awesome opportunity."

"But, why think of *me?*" Of course I had a major idea why, just wondered if he'd really tell me it was because I would never draw realistically. "Because we're buds?"

His eyebrows pulled toward each other. "Because your cartoon style—"

So he is in the same boat with Mr. Chun.

"—isn't just for graffiti art. I know that's what you might think—"

I let the flyer drop to the table, sat back, and crossed my arms. "How do you know what I think?"

"You're hanging out with Badalin, aren't you?"

I cocked my chin. "So telling me about this contest is supposed to get me to stop?"

"No. I don't know." He leaned back in his seat. "I was trying to show you a different track."

"Yeah, like how you asked me to be on the committee?"

"The committee?" When I didn't say anything else—like, *Yeah, remember? Because you felt sorry for me?*—he just looked away. "Just forget it, then. I didn't know you were going to be upset about this."

"I'm not." But I realized I was. Being so transparent irritated me. "Well, I didn't know you were going to tell me my art sucked, either." The minute I said it, I regretted it.

He jerked his attention back to my face. "*What* are you talking about?"

"Look, can I just get a ride home?" When he continued to gape at me like I'd just told him I was really a guy, I just shook my head. I never asked twice. "Forget it." I dug into my pocket and tossed down a ten.

"I'm not going to forget it. You're always telling me to forget stuff. When did I ever say your work sucked?"

His expression was so serious that it made me hesitate. He hadn't specifically said my work sucked. It was really just me and my own issues of relating the words "cartoony" and "whimsical" with being unskilled. Me, feeling like my art—

work sucked and that everyone else felt it, too. And it grated to be reminded of something that I couldn't change. That I'd never be close to anything like Nathan's style.

Real. Perfect.

So extremely talented.

I tried my best to forget the reality that I wasn't as gifted as I wanted to be, but at times like this, when someone whose talent I respected just shoved the truth in my face, there was no denying it. Miguel hadn't even told me if I was heading in the right direction with graffiti. I mean, I thought I was, but a girl needed confirmation. The other day I tried to put a fat cap on my spray can, but when I pressed the nozzle nothing came out. I shook the can and pressed, still nothing. Miguel finally told me the cap was clogged. That was kind of how I felt with my art, a spray can full of color and ideas ready to paint, but stuck—clogged—with no place to create.

No place for my art.

It all just *burned*.

But I couldn't tell Nathan any of this, so I just sat there, not saying anything, staring down at the cheese that congealed on my plate.

"This is bull," he muttered. He picked up my ten and tossed it back. "I got it, thanks." The "thanks" was so sharp it could have cut like an X-Acto knife.

We stood, Nathan's expression neutral—neither of us bothering to retrieve the flyer—and he motioned with his hand for me to go first.

Ticked off and still the nice guy. I didn't know how he pulled it off.

I walked down the aisle and turned down another toward the exit walkway, and—

Met eyes with Derek sitting in a booth.

His eyes slid behind me to Nathan, while mine moved to Petey, Mark . . .

. . . no Miguel.

. . . no Beth.

But there, with a giant burger in his hand, ketchup dripping down his chin, was Rock.

Mute was the key word to describe our conversation as Nathan drove his truck. The latest hit by Nelly played on the radio. But as we drove next to my neighborhood park, he pulled into the small parking lot. His headlights skimmed over the wooden North Caesar Park sign.

So fitting he should bring me here . . . a park that wasn't even a bleep on his mental radar and yet meant so much to me.

I glanced at him in the dark night, not knowing what to expect. He slid into a car slot and shut off the engine. The silence between us was so sudden, I could hear the *tick, tick* of the engine settling.

Clicking off his seat belt, he rested an arm up on the back of the bench seat, his fingers brushing my left shoulder.

My arms were crossed. Total defensive body language, I knew. Not because I was upset any longer, but because I knew he was pissed at me, and knowing that made me feel uncomfortable.

"This is North Caesar Park," he said quietly.

I nodded, looking out the windshield.

"Your neighborhood park."

I wasn't sure if it was a question but I didn't bother answering the obvious. I'd given him my address leaving the restaurant. He knew my street was around the corner.

He let out a breath. "Angel, don't go home mad."

His apologetic tone somehow released the tension in my body. "I'm not mad."

I was just reeling because I'd acted like a complete idiot and got upset at Nathan for my *own* insecurities, with a small part of me wondering why Beth and Miguel were MIA at the same time. The guys had all said "hi" to me at the restaurant. Derek had given me a mean, small smile. As if somehow I was doing something completely wrong and he was just so thrilled about it.

But I wasn't doing anything wrong. Hopefully I was about to do something right.

My palms grew damp because I knew I was going to have to tell Nathan something I didn't want to.

My inner fears. My deepest insecurities. If I wanted him to understand where I was coming from with my art—which I really did want to do.

But how to go about getting it all out when I never had before? Not even to Nana.

I uncrossed my arms, released my seat belt, and wiped my palms down the thighs of my jeans. "I'm sorry . . ."

"I'm the one who's sorry. I really was trying to do something nice for you, Angel. You're really talented. I don't want you to feel like I think your work sucks. That's bull."

I willed myself to look at him. "I know. It's not you, it's—"

His jaw twitched. "Badalin, right?"

I shook my head.

"You like him."

"No . . ." *Not as much as I like you.*

But that sounded pathetic. How to say in words that I thought I liked Miguel for his passion for his art and what he was willing to teach me? That as a potential boyfriend, he totally sucked? There were no words to make Nathan understand without me sounding like a total user.

His gaze drifted toward the windshield. "I didn't want to tell you about what happened between me and him before. Didn't want it to seem like I was trying to change your mind about being friends with him. Now I don't care. I just want you to know."

I kept my mouth shut, pushing my own confession away to save for later. I wanted badly to hear this.

"We used to be best friends in grade school."

When he paused for a moment, I filled in the silence. "I didn't know."

"Not many do. We lived on the same street and started

hanging out around second grade. For years we did everything together, especially when we both became interested in art. But there's stuff about Miguel, you just don't know . . . not my place to say, either."

It was the first time Nathan called Miguel by his first name, and it caught me off guard.

"Anyway," he continued. "Each year that passed he just wanted to push more limits with everything—rules, teachers, parents—with me by his side."

In a way, Miguel's actions made sense to me. Graffiti artists are known to push the envelope with their style.

"But once my dad saw how well I was doing in sports," Nathan continued, "he pushed me harder. Away from art and Miguel. Miguel, I don't know, resented me for not standing up to my dad. Our art went in different directions. Miguel had wanted me to learn graf with him, but it wasn't . . . me." He shrugged. "Then I moved with my family to another neighborhood, and we drifted apart.

"Once you don't go along with Miguel's way . . . it's like he can't forget. Ever since junior high he's tried to up me on something. Always a competition. I played along, but there was this girl I really liked. Her name was Tara, he made out with her while we were a couple."

"That must have been bad."

"Yeah, I was pissed." He smiled a little. "Hurt, too. I really liked this girl. First big crush, I guess. Miguel and I fought, kicked the crap out of each other. He never went out with her again. He'd just done it to get back at me for whatever he thought I did wrong. After that, I finally stopped caring what he did. Wasn't worth it anymore. He still cares, I guess."

After a moment, Nathan shifted closer to me. Even with just the moonlight as my only light source, I could still see the intense look in his eyes.

The look reminded me of when he was so focused on his artwork. And to have that much attention on me alone was like having a hundred butterflies fluttering under my skin.

"But I don't care what I have to do, Angel. I want you to be with me, not him."

My pulse drummed a solo beat.

"Not because you're hanging out with Miguel, but because I like you a lot. The person you are inside."

I was going all soft with his words. I licked my lips. *I don't like Miguel. I like you.*

He slid a warm hand to my cheek, the other resting on the knee of my jeans. His gaze dropped to my mouth. "You don't care what anyone says about your art—"

I hesitated. That was so *not* true. I did care.

"You're confident and true to yourself."

My eyes shifted away from his. No . . . I wasn't.

His hand slid up to my thigh, to finally rest on my hip. "Angel . . ."

I looked up.

His head was leaning toward mine and I didn't want him to stop.

My pulse scrambled. I closed my eyes and his mouth brushed mine. But that wasn't enough. Something inside me wanted more of him.

More of *something*.

Our mouths opened for a deeper kiss. I drew him closer to me. I couldn't believe this was happening.

I was kissing Nathan.

He was kissing me back.

Nothing else mattered at the moment. Not art, not graf, not the battle, not Miguel and Beth. Just me and Nathan, making out in his truck with the moonlight shining down on us at my favorite childhood park.

chapter eleven

CUTTING TIPS
A Technique to Change Caps into Fat Caps
    —Angel's Piecebook Notes
        (I felt like I was being forced to change.)

a man who sees you home and walks you to your door is a real man, Angel.

Nathan had walked me to my door. We'd kissed one last time before I walked into the house. My body was so warm. My skin felt like it was tingling. I put a finger to my lips. They were a little sore and soft at the same time.

Nathan wanted to see me again, like on a date.

I had to tell Beth.

I hesitated. Should I bring up her taking off with Miguel instead of hanging with me? Or act like nothing mattered?

Truthfully, I was in too good a mood to care about her ditching me right now.

I knocked on Nana's door, opened it, and told her I was home, then went back to the front room and grabbed the cordless to dial Beth's number. You could call pretty late at her mom's.

She answered on the third ring.

I sprawled out on the couch. "Beth, it's me. What are you doing?"

"Just watching TV."

"I had the best time with Nathan tonight." I went into the good details of the night, finishing off with the juicy stuff in the car and him wanting to see me again.

"That's cool, Angel," she countered, kind of mellow. "I'm really glad it went so well."

"Thanks . . ." But I couldn't help thinking, *That's it?*

This was a big thing for me. Where was the excitement she usually dished out? The overflow of eager questions? Beth was always interested about guys in general, especially when it involved lips and tongue.

I frowned, picking at the worn fabric at my knee. "So . . . what did you do at Miguel's?"

"Just hung out. Nothing really."

This was getting weirder by the second. Beth was usually busting with details. "Beth, what's up? What's the matter?"

"Nothing, just tired, you know?" A yawn sounded in my ear. "Can we talk tomorrow?"

"Yeah . . . okay."

"Talk to you later," she said. *Click.*

I turned off the phone. Since Beth was home now, she'd probably returned from Miguel's early tonight, right? She'd likely been home and Miguel off somewhere else while the guys were eating at Applebee's. Not, like, sitting next to her as we were talking on the phone or anything. Right?

I got up and changed into my jammies—a knee-length sleep shirt with Betty Boop shaking her butt—went to the bathroom, and washed my face and brushed my teeth, then curled under my covers and thought of Nathan.

Then Miguel . . .

I imagined the two of them as friends when they were little, then thought about how they acted so hostile to each other now. I'd had no idea they'd had such a past.

I had a problem, though.

How was I going to tell Miguel I was dating Nathan? Would he keep teaching me graffiti while I dated his number one enemy?

Wait a minute.

Nathan knew I was still going to hang out with Miguel and the crew, right?

The next night around 8:30, Miguel showed up at my house. He was dressed in all black: hooded sweatshirt, jeans, and his usual plain baseball cap.

I gave him a hesitant smile and swung open the screen door. "Hey, what's up?"

He cocked his head at me and flashed his crooked incisor. "Came to get you to come practice with the crew. Two more weeks till the battle."

A sense of relief settled inside me. This was the first time Miguel had smiled at me since the shot-down-his-kiss episode. This had to be a sign. Things were going to be cool between us now.

"All right." Yeah, I needed more practice writing. Big time. I hadn't moved up to actually piecing yet. Miguel had taught me there were pretty much three levels of graffiti. Tagging, throw-ups, and piecing. Besides, maybe this was the time to test the waters about Nathan, see how he felt about us hanging out. The guys had to have already told him they'd seen us out together. "I'll be out in a minute."

I slipped on my black hoodie, told Nana I'd be hanging out with some friends and would be back later, and I stepped out into the cool night. Nana hadn't questioned me. It was the weekend, no school tomorrow.

A chilly breeze pushed through the evening. Miguel's Blazer was parked under a streetlight. Music spilled out of the open windows along with the voices of the crew.

The passenger-side door swung open and Derek climbed out and shoved up his seat. He had a smirk on his round face that I ignored. Pulling my long ponytail over one shoulder, I hopped in and squished myself between Petey and Rock.

Rock took up one entire side to himself. Mateo was in the back area. He gave me a little wave.

Everyone said, "What's up?" I couldn't really have a conversation with anyone as we drove away because Miguel raised the volume of Bone Thugs to boom through the Blazer.

I was a little surprised Beth wasn't with us. Obviously she'd been hanging with the crew without me. I thought to ask Miguel or Derek, but figured my voice would be drowned out by the music.

When Miguel turned down a main street in the opposite direction of his house, nerves tickled my stomach. I'd assumed we'd be practicing on the boards at his house.

I leaned toward Petey, his yellow hair spikes brushing my face. "Where are we going?" I asked, kind of loud.

He leaned closer. "Huh!?"

I rolled my eyes. "WHERE ARE WE GOING?"

"OH! YOU'LL SEE."

I sat back and reached up to tug at the skin on my bottom lip. Minutes passed as I pulled on the same dumb piece of dead skin that wouldn't budge—there was actually a technique to lip peeling so you wouldn't make your lips bleed—when we drove into the industrial side of town, where a lot of old mechanic shops and yards with old machinery were located.

Miguel finally pulled into a graveled lot with a few other cars. The music was lowered and the engine shut off.

"Miguel," I was finally able to say. "What are we doing? I thought we were going to practice writing."

He didn't look at me as he opened his door. "We are. After."

"After what?"

"Need some supplies." He stepped out of the car.

Derek pushed the seat forward. Rock got out, then me. I scooted forward and looked out the door to see a lit-up old two-story rusted warehouse that was about three houses in length. Music drifted out from a garage door that was halfway up. This wasn't your typical local paint store.

My stomach felt a little light. This side of town was dead on a Saturday night, making this place feel secluded and un-safe. "I'll just wait here."

Derek laughed. "She's scared."

Petey whispered beside me, "I don't always like it here, ei-ther. But, you know, we're just picking stuff up. Then outtie."

I looked at Petey's face. He seemed sincere. I did *not* want to go into that warehouse, but I was here and I felt like Miguel was testing me. As if asking, *Are you really tough enough to be with the crew?*

Well, I was. Wanted to be. "He comes here if the stores are closed. This guy sells Miguel any colors he wants, even dif-ferent caps."

"Fine." Resigned, I got out of the Blazer, pulled the hood over my head, stuffed my hands in my front pocket, and walked with the crew toward the warehouse. The gravel crunched under our feet. My head told me I was making a total wrong move.

We ducked beneath the garage door. A radio played what sounded like hard rock throughout the large warehouse. One, two, three old rusted cars were jacked up on stands to the far right, dirty car parts thrown on floors and shelves. A scent of oil and gas assaulted my nostrils. A couple of young Latino guys were kicked back on a torn couch, holding large forty-ounce beers in their hands.

One of them nodded at Miguel.

I kept my head low, not making eye contact with anyone, and followed Miguel and the crew into a connecting office. Inside was more crap spread out on the floor and shelves. Cigarette smoke clouded the interior. In the center was a desk spotted with beer cans with three older guys playing cards. Yeah, older as in adult, as in men.

Right then, I wanted to turn and walk away. I didn't trust men. Growing up with my mom's endless line of boyfriends, I'd met and seen all kinds. Some not so friendly, some way too friendly. Men were not to be trusted. Men drinking alcohol, even more.

Mierda. My hands clenched into sweaty fists inside my sweatshirt. I didn't want to draw attention to myself as being the only girl with a room full of guys. I wanted this done and over. I wanted to go home.

Miguel stepped forward and knocked fists with a man with a long mustache that curved down the sides of his mouth. They started speaking in Spanish, too fast for me to understand. Something about paint and tonight.

The man looked straight at me and I knew I wasn't unnoticed anymore. They kept talking and the man kept staring. My stomach felt seriously twisted. *Damn, damn, damn.* Get me out of here.

"Let's bail," I whispered to Petey. At the moment, he was the only one who felt as uneasy as I did. In my book, that made us best buds.

His eyes shifted to me, but he didn't say anything. It was almost as if he was afraid to speak.

The man threw down his cards and rose to his feet, his eyes still on me. My pulse sped up. My hands were sweating. He walked toward me. I kept my eyes on his bloated chest and stepped back. He walked right by me and relief hit me so fast, I felt nauseated. Sick.

Miguel followed and I fell behind, feeling like a zombie. Followed them to a large cabinet of spray cans.

Cans of different colors. Containers of different caps. Money exchanged.

Loaded up, we walked out of the garage.

My eyes were glued on the Blazer so I wouldn't look back. I didn't relax until I was seated in my seat again, packed tight next to Petey and Rock.

Miguel started the engine, music blasted our ears, and he drove.

I didn't care which direction we were headed in this time. Relief was slowly seeping through my body. Things could have gone bad in a half-dozen different ways, but everything went okay. It all made me wonder if there was a point to bringing me to that garage tonight. Had I been right? Was Miguel trying to test me to see if I'd freak out as the only girl? Obviously I wasn't the only one who felt uncomfortable going there. Petey had felt uneasy, too. Or was there no point at all and it was just Miguel not caring how anyone felt but himself?

A few minutes later, Miguel cruised the Blazer along a wooded boundary layered with a metal fence, tall pine trees hovering on the other side. We were at the back of East Mason Park, the only park in town that was also used for skating, with its cemented hills and walls.

No one said anything as we piled out. A strange tingle started in my gut. A little uneasiness and a little excitement. More and more this night made me feel as if I was being tested. How much more would I have to do to prove my loyalty to the crew?

I slid to the door and got out. The wind had picked up enough to whip my ponytail around like a live snake. Miguel opened the back end and Mark hit the ground on his feet. They started taking out backpacks.

Packs that suspiciously rattled.

My stomach sank.

This wasn't another stop before Miguel's house.

The crew was not only practicing, but on public property. A park. City domain. Which made this against the law. Didn't matter that it was one of the richer neighborhoods. It wasn't ever cool to mess with places where little kids came to play. Wasn't right.

I walked toward Miguel. He grabbed the rim of his baseball cap and slid it around so that he wore his cap backward, and finally met my eyes. The Blazer's interior light illuminated his face. He smiled. Not a very nice one, either. It was that smug curve of his lips I'd seen on him before. I didn't like it much.

"Why didn't you tell me?" I asked him straight out. But you know, I had this small idea that Miguel really was ticked I'd been with Nathan last night, and him not telling me about this "surprise" was some form of retaliation.

"What?"

He knew what I was talking about, but he wasn't making this easy. "Fine, be that way, *Jack*." He didn't like me calling him that, but hey, I could be pissed off, too. You've heard of freedom of speech? Freedom to be pissed off, and all that. I crossed my arms against the cold. "But I'm not doing this."

His smile fell away. "Yeah. You are."

The guys started to climb the fence. The fence and cans rattled together.

"No. I'm not."

"I knew it." His words were layered with disgust.

I shifted, tiny dried pine needles crunching beneath my K-Swisses. "What?"

"You're a friggin' toy."

I flinched.

Derek was still around. He snorted. The jerk.

Miguel shook his head. "You talk like you want to be a real writer, then you back down when it's time to prove yourself. You play at graf like a scribbler. You think if you piece a board in a backyard that makes you a writer?" He curled his lip. "Get real."

After all the emotions I held in tonight, I felt pumped. Amped. Who the hell did he think he was calling me out? Who made him frigging king? I was tired of hanging on his every word, trying to search for some wisdom about a style of art he was barely teaching me. I was tired of this night and wanted it to end. "You know what? Shove it up your ass!"

Miguel smirked, like my attitude was amusing him.

The hell with that. I wasn't here to amuse anyone. "That's it. I'm done. I'm done with *you*. Done with the crew. And definitely done with your stupid-ass battle." I sounded cocky, so sure. But deep inside, a part of me wondered if I was doing the right thing.

Miguel stepped forward. "You're what?"

I tilted my chin up. "You heard me."

"Then be prepared to get your ass beat down, *chica.*"

I looked him up and down. "By who?"

"West Coast Vandals." He glanced toward Derek. "I guess Angel doesn't know about the rule of backing out of a battle between our crews."

"Guess not," Derek agreed.

My patience was gone. *"What rule?"*

"One crew member backs down, they're marked by the other crew to get beat down. Anywhere, anytime. They find you, they slam you. Don't matter if you say you're a member of the crew or not."

"Bullshit."

He let out a little laugh, shrugged a shoulder. "Don't believe me, but don't come cryin' to me when it happens."

My back teeth rubbed together. This was not cool. So unfair. Yeah, I believed Miguel about the rule. I knew my hands were tied and it sucked hard. Violence was all around us, at school, on the streets. In the graf world I was slowly learning about, where the only rules were about freedom of art, it made sense anything could happen, even a beatdown.

Besides all this ignorant crap tonight, deep within I still craved to be a *real* graf artist. To find my place in the art world. But maybe I was so pissed because Miguel was right. I'd just been playing at graffiti. Living in some mental reality that Miguel and the guys *didn't* really go out and bomb the town illegally. That writing at Miguel's house and entering some battles was as good as it got. Now standing here in the cold faced with the truth . . . I didn't know what I wanted. Didn't know what to do.

Would I break the law? Deface this rich neighborhood park to become a graf writer?

Or would I forever live in my own personal *Toy* Land?

With all these uncertainties there was something I *did* know for a change. If I didn't do what Miguel wanted, he would walk away from me. Let me get jumped by the other crew. Maybe even leave my ass here in the night, miles from my side of town, without a ride home.

This was the way Miguel worked.

I walked to the fence and dug my fingers through the iron octagons. Once I climbed this fence there was no going back. I knew that.

Taking a breath, I climbed.

My heart pounded. Pounded so hard, I thought it might vibrate my whole body.

I'd found my spot about six feet away from Miguel. Petey was to the right of me, already arching his arm above his head, spraying the cemented wall. The hiss of the can filled the air.

My hood was pulled over my head, the wind chilling my face. I had a pack full of spray cans, a couple of caps in my pocket. There wasn't much light. The park was closed at sunset.

I was a novice here. I knew that. It was best to start simple.

Licking my lips, I pulled out my lightest color. Pale green.

I held the can and pressed the nozzle, moving my hand quickly. I began to create lines—an outline of my piece to come. But again, I sprayed too close. A small line of paint ran down the wall. "Damn."

"Car," rang out with a harsh whisper.

I whipped my head toward Miguel, saw him on the ground, and flattened myself on the cement.

My breaths filtered out of my mouth. The cement was

cold and rough beneath my hands and face. Headlights flashed quickly over Miguel's body. If anyone jumped up and ran for the fence, I wouldn't be far behind.

A moment later, Miguel was back on his feet. Cans were rattling.

I shut my eyes, blew out a breath, then got back on my feet. Picked up my can and began again.

Time flew by as I painted and created. The fact that I was breaking the law, marring the walls of a public park, was buried under the excitement and freedom of creating a piece. No rules. No guidelines. Just me and my thoughts, my skill. My art coming from my hand.

I felt so free. More than I ever had before. And this was a feeling to be cherished.

I stepped back, my hands almost numb now from the cold, my fingers tired. My eyes had adjusted to the dark long ago. In the distance I could hear crickets chirping. Someone dropped a can on the ground.

Before me was my first piece.

"GRAFANGL" in purple, green, and black. A sombrero tilted sideways on top of the "G," a bright halo above the hat. Feathered white wings sprang out on either side of my tag, with a few floating feathers in the air as if they'd fallen from the wings.

Far from perfect, but I was damn proud of it.

There was a flash to my left. Petey was taking pics with a small digital cam.

"That's awesome, Angel," he said.

I smiled. "Thanks."

Miguel called out, "Let's bail."

I stood there a moment more, then gathered my empty cans into my pack.

In the car, we were all quiet. The music beat around us and it was the first time I felt so comfortable with the crew. I leaned my head against Petey, who sat next to me. You'd think the adrenaline rush would be making us talk, fidget, but it was as if we were all so tired from putting a bit of ourselves into our pieces. And it connected us, in a way I'd never felt with any other artists before.

This would be a moment I would remember for the rest of my life.

At 1:34 a.m., Miguel dropped me home. Cold. Tired. And smelling of the strong odor of spray paint. The minute the screen door squeaked on its hinges, the front door swung open. My mom stood before me in sweats and a T-shirt, her shoulders raising up and down, her face stiff with a totally pissed-off look.

"Get your butt in here *now*."

Mom reached out and pulled me over the threshold of our home by my sweatshirt. I yanked away from her. I was in deep crap. Curfew wasn't really regulated in this house. If I stayed out late, I was usually out in the neighborhood, not far from a call-out. If I knew I was going to be out late to party, I just crashed at Beth's. So when Nana or my mom hadn't been able to find me, they likely became worried. I could understand that, but I was tired and didn't want to deal with this now.

Mom shut and locked the door. The sudden warmth of the house made a small shiver travel down my back. I glanced at Nana sitting on her old recliner. She scooted forward and pushed up with her cane. "Now that I know you are okay, *m'ija,* I'm going to bed." She looked tired and guilt weighed on my shoulders.

"Sorry, Nana," I murmured to her as she passed. She reached out and patted me on the shoulder and continued to her room.

"You better have a good explanation, Angel, and I mean *good,*" my mother said.

I blew out a breath and rolled my eyes as I turned to face her. But I froze when I saw the envelope in her hand. My envelope. My art money stash.

"That's mine!" I reached out a hand and she pulled her hand out of reach. "Now you're going through my stuff? That's bullsh—"

Mom put a finger in front of my face. "Don't you say it. I have every right to go through my couch *and* your stuff when you just take off at all hours of the night. I was a teenager, too, Angel, I know you're probably out partying and drinking. You're lucky I didn't call the cops. You're lucky nothing happened to you." She shook the envelope at me. "Where did you get this money?"

"I earned it. It's mine."

"You earned it? The only way you could have gotten this is if you're selling dope or you stole it. Which is it?"

My mouth opened with a harsh laugh as I tilted my head toward the ceiling. "Whatever. You're crazy. I don't know the kind of guys you're screwing, but you got me all wrong."

The flash of her hand didn't register until it collided with my face.

I stepped back, cradling the sting of my cheek. Tears sprung to my eyes. Something flickered on her face—sadness, guilt?—before she turned away toward the hallway. She threw the envelope at the couch. Bills floated to the cushions.

My face heated. "I hate you! You never understand me!"
You never care.

Pain and hurt spread from my gut, to chest, to throat.

I'm not going to cry.

I'm not going to cry.

I sniffed and walked to the couch, falling down on my back, fighting tears. *I won't cry over her anymore.* There were all these emotions spinning around inside my head, in my chest, and in my gut. I stared at the ceiling and I concentrated on burying ever last one, as if I were a bottle and I could trap all my emotions with a cork on top so that I felt nothing.

I was so tired, my body went numb and I just lay there thinking nothing, feeling nothing until my eyes grew heavy and closed.

chapter twelve

FAME
What a Writer Gets
When His Work Is Seen Everywhere
> —Angel's Piecebook Notes
> *(Even where you DON'T want it to be.)*

Monday morning I walked out of my house, slamming the door. My mood was always shot on Mondays but coming off of a weekend of not speaking to my mom even though she was in the same room with me was the biggest drag of all. We hadn't looked at each other, or even tried to speak. We were like passing ghosts.

I wasn't paying attention as I stepped onto the last step to the walkway, and like an idiot, I tripped over the dumb newspaper and fell on the small walkway on my knees and hands.

"Stupid, stupid, *stupid*!" I slapped at the concrete in frustration while my knees stung. I got up and sat on the last step, digging my fingers into my hair and leaning my elbows on my thighs.

The rubber band had snapped off the rolled paper and the newspaper curved open. I caught sight of a grainy photo of something colorful and familiar . . .

I leaned forward and grabbed the paper, flattening it open on my lap.

"Mierda," I whispered. My scalp tingled with the beginnings of nervous perspiration.

There on the front page of the local paper was a picture of the piece—"GRAFANGL"—I painted at East Mason Park Saturday night, right beside Miguel's "BADMAN."

Under the headline: "Is Homestead Graffiti Vandalism on the Rise?"

I read further . . .

Under investigation . . . vandals will be fined and prosecuted. . . . If anyone has any information, please contact the Homestead Police . . .

I was so screwed.

"Hi, Angel," Beth murmured to me at our lockers.

I just nodded my head, barely looking at her, but I didn't care. Beth and I hadn't exactly been living up to our friendship roles lately.

Not even enough to comment on the latest hickeys that had sprouted on her neck over the weekend. Apparently she and Derek had gone at it again. But that information had nothing on the news I'd read in the morning paper—on the front frigging page. What did I expect for small-town Homestead? Kids were actually waving the front page around school, pinning up the picture on the bulletin board. It took serious willpower not to reach up and rip it down. The bombing we did on the park *was* big headlines. In the darkened night, I hadn't known how much damage we'd done.

And yeah—no matter how much it grated to say it—from the other pictures I saw in the paper, it *did* look like a mess. Maybe not Miguel's or my piece, but the pieces by the other crew, were just plain chaotic with jerky lines, uneven lettering, and tacky colors.

In the heat of the moment, the bombing at the park had felt like art, but today it just felt like . . . vandalism.

What if I got caught? What if someone saw us? I'd be in serious trouble if the police found out. All of us would.

"Angel, you okay? You look . . . pale?"

I turned to Beth. She looked hesitant, uncertain. I leaned close and told her.

Everything.

She jerked back, eyes wide. "Holy shit."

I placed my hand on her shoulder. "Don't say a word to *anyone*."

She nodded her head, blonde curls brushing her shoulders. "I wouldn't. I swear."

Letting it all out, I felt a little better. Not totally, but enough to relax somewhat.

Now the only thing I had to worry about was someone from the crew blabbing his mouth. Because there was no way I wanted to be caught. "Fined" or "prosecuted." My mom would flip. I'd be kicked off the mural committee.

I'd gain the reputation of being a vandal instead of a graffiti artist.

And I couldn't forget about Nathan. I had no idea what he would do . . .

After fourth period, I stuffed my pack in my locker. I didn't even want to think about the bio paper and geometry test I'd just failed. Right now they weren't on the top of my list of worries. I hadn't crossed paths with any of the crew, but I needed to talk to them. Seriously. To talk to Miguel about the news article. Find out what he thought. Was he freaking out about getting caught like I was?

But when I whirled around to rush to the parking lot to see if I could head anyone off before going to lunch, I rammed right into a warm chest.

Nathan caught me against him.

I gripped his arms and raised my gaze to his face.

His eyebrows were furrowed, his mouth in a straight line. His hazel eyes almost accusing.

"What?" I asked. "What's wrong?"

He looked away. "We need to talk."

I licked my dry lips. This couldn't be good. "Sure." My hunt for Miguel would have to wait.

I searched around. Where was Beth? Maybe I could have her deliver a message to Miguel that I needed to talk to him later. But she wasn't around.

Nathan gripped my hand, lacing our fingers, and started to the parking lot. I had the strangest rush holding hands with him in school. But not knowing what was going on sort of took the glow out of the moment.

When we reached Nathan's truck, there was no sign of the crew or Miguel's ride. They had likely already taken off to lunch.

We got into Nathan's truck and he drove off school campus.

"Where are we going?"

"My house."

Ten minutes of strained silence later, we drove onto a street with two-story homes with beautiful large yards. I squirmed in my seat as we pulled into a circular driveway of a peach-colored home.

"This is where you live?" I asked, staring up at the large front yard and patio with benches and potted plants. Of course, I had an idea his neighborhood would be the opposite of mine—so clean, so nice, so out of my league—but seeing it drove home the reality.

He nodded.

I tried to ignore the curl of discomfort in my chest, but there just was no way to do it. I decided to be silent until he was ready to spring whatever was eating him.

We got out and made our way inside his house and I tried not to gawk at the stylish, classy furniture in the front room. And the house had a nice smell to it. Something lemony. We passed another room as he took me down a hallway. I had a quick glimpse of an entire wall filled with shelves of trophies. We passed photos on the wall, of a younger Nathan and his sister when they were in grade school.

We climbed a curving staircase and then turned a corner to a closed doorway. He opened the door and ushered me in first.

His bedroom.

It wasn't filled with dirty gym socks or clothes everywhere, but neat and clean. The double bed was neatly made and covered with a dark navy comforter. I wondered if he made his bed himself. But then I recalled the fresh lemony scent and figured a maid probably took care of it. A black drafting table was set in the right corner with a couple of school books on top. Markers and colored pencils were lined against the wall.

And his beautiful artwork was framed and hanging on his walls. I walked toward the frames, reaching out a finger to lightly touch the black frame. The painting was of a young girl standing on a sandy beach, her hand tapping the water.

The detail of the ripples of the waves made the painting so realistic.

I blinked when I realized his work hadn't been in the parts of the house I had seen.

"How could you do it?" he shot out.

I spun around to face him, my whole body filling with anxiety. *He knew about us bombing the park.*

I swallowed. "Who told you?"

"Who do you think?" He scanned my face. "So it's true?" He didn't give me time to answer. He turned away, rubbing the back of his neck.

Stuffing my hands in the pocket of my hoodie, I scraped my teeth across my bottom lip.

He turned back to me. His face looked hurt.

"I don't know what to say . . ."

"I thought you understood what kind of person he is," he said.

"He's my friend, Nathan. They all are. I wanted Miguel to teach me graf. I didn't know the park was in the plans."

He shook his head. "What are you talking about? I don't care about graffiti right now, Angel. I'm talking about you kissing Miguel."

chapter **thirteen**

TO BUFF
To Remove
      —Angel's Piecebook Notes
      (Disappear . . . like I wish I could.)

I stood there, trying to shift from believing Nathan was accusing me of vandalism, to his actually accusing me of making out with another guy.

Miguel had told Nathan I'd kissed him.

Call me slow, but had I been nothing but another competition in the rivalry between Nathan and Miguel that had started way back in junior high? There wasn't any reason for Miguel to tell Nathan about a kiss that had taken place a week ago *unless* he wanted to hurt Nathan, and the relationship Nathan and I had just begun. I should have realized this before, but I'd been so wrapped up within my own wants and insecurities that I hadn't seen the big picture flashing before my eyes like a wide-screen flick.

Miguel was such a first-class *prick*.

Hold on. Nathan had asked me out *after* I started hanging with Miguel. Was Nathan's interest only generated by Miguel's interest?

I quickly kicked that thought to the curb. Nathan was so not like Miguel. And I couldn't forget about Friday night in his truck at the park. Nathan had told me straight out he liked me for *me*, not for any ulterior motives.

Whether he liked the *real* me was another matter.

"Aren't you going to say anything?" Nathan asked quietly. It seemed my stunned reaction somehow calmed him. He stuffed his hands in the pockets of his faded jeans and leaned up against his wall.

I nodded. "Yeah. Just wondering if you're going to believe me over Miguel."

He lifted his eyebrows. "Are you saying he's lying?"

"In a way . . ."

He shook his head. "Do better than that, Angel."

"All right. Yeah. I kissed him—once—before I kissed you. Before we went out Friday night. That's the truth."

He was silent for a moment. "For real?"

"I wouldn't lie about this."

"When he told me, it was hard to believe. But you

know, he'd gone out with a girl I liked before, why not again?"

"I see where you're coming from. I do. But I'm not like that other girl."

He met my eyes. "I didn't mean to compare you two."

I nodded. Since we were being all honest . . . "Can I ask you something?"

He lifted a shoulder. "Go ahead."

"Did you tell Miguel you only asked me onto the mural committee because you felt I would never get on it without you? That you felt sorry for me—"

"Hell, no." His expression wavered with shock. "Is that what he told you?"

I lifted my eyebrows in acknowledgment.

"Looks like we were both had." He blew out a frustrated breath. "Why do you hang out with him, Angel?"

I gave him the only answer I could. "He's my ride to the place I want to go with my art."

Expression.

Freedom.

Recognition.

This was my chance to come clean . . . about my inner havoc with my art. "I know how you feel about Miguel, and now that he's done this—" how he maneuvered me into breaking the law, took me where I never wanted to go—"I know he's not a true friend. But graf style, it's something special. Something I really enjoy." Okay, so maybe that wasn't totally explaining why I wanted to learn graffiti so badly, but I couldn't tell him why right now. Just *couldn't*.

Especially the part about vandalizing the park and the battle I still needed to compete in. What would Nathan think of me once he found out I was part of that mess? Would he still want me as a friend? Still want to date me?

I wasn't ready to find out.

Nathan finally curved his lips, relief flickering across his face. "I should have known something was up when he told me. I'd feel better if you hadn't kissed him at all, but . . ." He shrugged. "I can't hold it against you if it happened before we started hanging out. But Angel, now that we are, don't let it happen again."

I swallowed. "What are you saying? That you don't want me to date anyone else?"

He reached up and rubbed the back of his neck. "Yeah. We don't know where this will go, but let's be up-front with each other."

So he wasn't asking us to be together officially like boyfriend and girlfriend, but to date only each other. I could handle that. "Agreed."

He met my eyes across the five feet of light blue and white weaved carpet that separated us. It was as if he wanted to say something more.

Something important.

But whatever it was, he never said. He pushed off the wall and walked toward me.

My heartbeats picked up.

Our arms slid around each other and we kissed. He was solid, so strong against me. Not the first time, I noticed the subtle cologne he wore that was starting to become familiar.

And we kissed . . .

He pulled back and smiled, his fingers playing with my hair behind my back. "We'd better get back."

My gaze flicked down to the front of his cotton white T-shirt. "Yeah." Back to school, back to all my problems. He released me, opening the bedroom door. As I was about to walk out, I spotted a watercolor painting hanging on the wall.

The scene consisted of an elderly Mexican woman wearing a poncho, sitting in a rocking chair with a small swaddled infant in her arms. Light streamed through the window as she stared down at the baby with a soft serene expression.

The detail was outstanding for a watercolor. The woman's skin was dark and etched with age.

And it nearly took my breath.

"Nathan . . . it's beautiful."

"Thanks."

I looked at him. His cheeks were flooded with color. How could he be so bashful of his talent? "I never seen you work with Mexican culture before. I didn't think . . ."

"That I had it in me?"

I smiled, but I was embarrassed. "I don't know."

"I value my roots, Angel, just like you."

That was good to know.

We walked out.

Nathan's lips against mine just a moment ago, and how close I felt to him right now, made it hard to concentrate on Miguel at all.

Just as we were about to head out Nathan's front door, the lock clicked and the door swung open. Nathan's dad, wearing a dark business suit and pin-striped tie, stood in the doorway.

Nerves tickled under my skin as we stood there in the quiet. Some parents had this big *thing* about being home alone without having adult supervision and I didn't know how Nathan's dad would react.

"Hey, Dad," Nathan said, pressing a hand to my back as if to move me along. But I resisted, because—hello?—that was difficult with his dad blocking the exit.

"M'ijo," his dad said in a low voice. "I didn't expect you home."

"Yeah, thought I forgot something. Had to run by and check during my lunch."

His dad slowly looked at our clothes. What did he think? We'd come here for a quick roll in Nathan's bed?

Nathan smiled. "But the textbook wasn't here, either. Must have left it in a class. You remember, Angel."

Mr. Ramos offered his large dark hand.

I had no choice but to shake it—which was bad because my dumb palms were damp. Nathan's dad was a little intimidating with his tall body in an expensive-looking suit. A far cry from any man my mom had dated before. Where my mom's boyfriends were so bland I could barely tell them apart, Mr. Ramos had the presence to command a room.

"Nice to see you again, Angel." He checked his gold wristwatch. "You'd better get back to school, *m'ijo*."

"On our way now."

"Practice after school?"

Something strange flickered across Nathan's face. "Mural committee."

Mr. Ramos's lips firmed. "I see." He looked at me as if to say something not so great about the committee. But before he could say whatever he was about to, I shifted my feet. On purpose.

His gaze drifted to my self-decorated tennis shoes, and he sighed. He had to know he wasn't going to get me as an ally. "I'll see you at dinner."

We said our good-byes and walked out the door to Nathan's truck. I couldn't help wondering what was up with parents against art? Was there some kind of secret organization? Or was it just Nathan's dad and my mom who stood out from all the rest?

"So we'll meet in the courtyard after school?" Nathan asked as we shuffled out of fifth period.

"Sounds good," I said.

"Nathan, you ready to run?"

I stilled. Misty—perky, pretty, ex-girlfriend—Peterson.

"Hey, Misty. Yeah." Nathan turned to me and smiled. "I'll meet you there."

I nodded.

But I couldn't really do anything about Nathan being with his ex. Nathan and I weren't officially boyfriend/girlfriend. And was I really *that* insecure that I couldn't handle them running together?

Misty smiled at me. Nice.

I smiled back, wishing I didn't have to force mine to be so friendly, then they ambled off, looking like the perfect teen couple. Reminding me that Nathan and I probably looked like total opposites together. I wasn't completely sure what he saw in me. Where he thought our relationship would go. Truthfully, I didn't think it would last long. Our lives were so different, as was the direction of our art. Nathan's talent would surely pave his future, and I couldn't see that happening for me.

"Move it, Angel. You're blocking the doorway." Miguel brushed past me. He had only smirked in my direction during class. This was the first opportunity I had to get him alone.

Rock sidled up to us.

Miguel was about to take off, but I latched on to his arm. He raised his eyebrows and looked at my hand.

"I need to talk to you for a minute." My tone definitely wasn't polite.

He smiled like he knew something was up. "Yeah, what?"

I released him and moved over to a secluded corner. He followed, while Rock leaned against some lockers and waited.

I took a breath and asked Miguel what the heck we were going to do about being wanted by the police.

He laughed like I'd just told him the funniest joke in the world.

A real riot.

"This is serious," I said. I didn't know if I was trying to convince him or me.

He shook his head. "The cops aren't going to find out unless you tell them. Don't worry about it."

"What do you mean 'me'? What about the rest of the crew?" I hadn't forgotten about the pics taken that night, either. "How do I know they won't tell someone? Or someone who knows you figures out it was you?"

"Who? Like other graf writers? Damn, you got a lot to learn. Nothing's gonna happen. No one's gonna tell. There's a code. We don't narc on each other no matter what. Chill."

Yeah, I probably was being uncool, getting in his face. Being all nervous-like. But this was my life and rep we were talking about here.

Apparently he thought the conversation was finished because he started to walk down the hall with Rock by his side.

Exasperated, I followed. I needed to tell Miguel so many things. That all this breaking the law wasn't cool. Wasn't me.

That he was the biggest jerk for telling Nathan about our kiss.

"Miguel—"

He came to an abrupt stop and pivoted toward me. His forehead was creased, his eyes annoyed. "Drop it, all right? You're making a big deal out of nothin'."

Nothing? Was he crazy?

Rock gave me a look that said, *Just leave it alone.*

So against my need to tell Miguel a whole boatload more, I backed off and they continued down the hall. In a way, Rock was right. I didn't want to make a scene in the middle of student traffic. Someone could hear and high school drama wasn't what I was usually about, not that you'd ever know it from the way I was acting.

Maybe if I just ignored all of it, it would all go away.

Yeah, I could just not look back on the incident and no one would be the wiser. I could erase from my mind being wanted by the cops. Being a part of Miguel's nefarious plot against Nathan.

Sure, sounded nice, but in reality world? Wasn't going to happen.

But I did know I wasn't going to do any bombing like this again. Vandalism was wrong, the repercussions too big. I scanned the sea of passing kids and caught sight of Beth. I raised my hand to get her attention. Funny thing, though, I could have sworn she caught my eye, but maybe she didn't because she swerved around a corner and disappeared.

I remembered our phone conversation again and how Beth acted so weird. She'd seemed okay when we had talked this morning, but she'd been nowhere to be found right before lunch. Which was stranger still since we always hung out at lunch.

Yeah, my life wasn't exactly walking an easy road here, but something was up with Beth and I needed to know what. We had sixth-period economics together. No way she could avoid me any longer.

Economics class was about to end. I'd been stealing quick looks at Beth all period. She looked okay from what I could see, but we were two rows away from each other. Malone and Rodriguez didn't often sit next to each other in classes where teachers lived by their attendance book.

Mr. Torres was barking out something about a homework reading assignment, but my attention was on Beth when she rose with her binder and book and started walking toward the back of the class. She also carried a pencil in her hand as she made her way toward the wall sharpener.

I frowned. Then the bell rang and suddenly Beth slipped right out the door.

"That's it," I muttered under my breath. I zipped up my pack and scrambled out toward the door, squeezing between kids.

"Hey, chill out, Angel," someone said.

"Watch where you're going," some girl named Lisa snapped.

"Sorry, all right?" I careened around the corner toward our lockers.

Beth was already shutting hers closed.

"Beth! Hold up!"

Weird, but when she finally looked at me, it was as if she was about to face a ticked-off principal or something. Her shoulders were slumped, her expression sort of . . . sad?

I shook my head as I walked toward her. "Beth, you *have* to tell me what's wrong."

She opened her mouth, then closed it.

"Beth. Be real. There is something wrong. I'm your best friend. Just tell me what's up."

Beth's eyes glistened. Her mouth tightened.

My eyes widened.

I quickly opened my locker and stuffed in my pack, slammed the door shut, and swung an arm around her shoulders before guiding her down the hall toward the front of the school. I didn't know where to take her, other than to start walking to her house. Students were pretty much taking off for the day, but we needed privacy. My stomach was twisting. I was kind of scared. I didn't think I'd ever seen Beth this upset before.

"You okay?" I asked her.

She nodded and sniffed. I took my arm off her and we walked for a bit.

After a couple of blocks, I couldn't deal with the suspense anymore. "Spill, Beth. What's happened?"

Beth stopped.

I stopped.

She looked down at the sidewalk, one arm holding her binder and textbook, her free hand tugging at the hem of her shirt. "I . . ."

"*What?*"

"I—*wentoutwithMiguel.*"

chapter fourteen

BITE
To Mimic Another Writer's Style
        —Angel's Piecebook Notes
        (Totally not cool.)

I blinked. "You what?"

But I'd heard her. Beth had just told me she'd gone out with Miguel.

She took off again, her shoulders slumped, her head lowered.

I finally shook off enough of my surprise to follow. "When?"

"Friday, when I went to his house."

I nodded. When she'd ditched me to go with him. Glancing at her neck, I understood the hickeys weren't from Derek, but from Miguel. Couldn't really pin down a certain emotion. I had a lot of them. But the main discomfort was that even though I had kissed Miguel just once, Beth and I had this belief that friends didn't date guys their friends had gone out with. A pact wasn't made, but we'd seen it happen with friends around school and actually talked about how we'd never do that to each other. And the fact that she didn't even care about what I would think about her going out with Miguel made me wonder what kind of friendship we had.

Was that why Beth had been avoiding me? Or had something worse happened . . .

"Beth, did Miguel do something that you didn't like? Did he—"

"No, nothing like that." She blew out a breath. "I went out with him because hot guys like him don't usually go for me. I kissed him because I liked him. I kissed him because . . ."

Beth stopped walking. She pivoted toward me.

Her blue eyes were tearing, her cheeks pink.

I swallowed hard.

"I kissed him to get back at *you*."

I shook my head. "Why? What did I do?"

"*Because*, Angel. You may not believe it, but you always have the attention from guys. And you know, I've accepted that. I mean, you are my best friend. But all of a sudden you're so into him and his dumb graffiti. And then all of a sudden you're *in* his crew. And you didn't even tell me. If we're supposed to be such best friends, how come you didn't tell me?"

I lifted my hands. "I was going to, but then the guys told you before I could. I was going to talk to you about it—"

"But, yeah, you didn't. I felt left out. Or maybe I was just tired of *you* getting all the attention all the time."

I gave her an irritated look. "Why do you keep saying that? *What* attention?"

"Do I have to spell it out? You're thin. You're pretty. I'm not."

"Don't be dumb, Beth. You're not fat, if that's what you're trying to say, and you *are* pretty. You go out with guys all the time."

Her eyes narrowed. "So what, I'm a slut?"

"That's not what I mean. You just, you know, go out with guys a lot."

"So what about you? First going out with Miguel, then straight to Nathan. Trying to follow in your mom's footsteps or what?"

That pissed me off. "Shut up, Beth. As if you have any room to talk about *my* mom."

Her face reddened. "Maybe I am like my mom because you know what else?" Beth was yelling now.

"*What?*" I yelled back.

"Me and Miguel did it," she spat out, eyes narrowed. "Something you've never even done."

I faltered for half a second. "Big—freaking—deal, Beth! Good for you. What do you want me to say?"

Why am I the bad guy here? She was the one who'd screwed someone I'd been interested in first.

"To think I looked up to you," she said almost absently. "I thought you were a good friend for me. What was I thinking?"

That stopped me cold.

I felt a stiffness in my shoulders, as if a giant art clip was pitching my muscles. "Look, Beth. I didn't twist your arm to be with Miguel, all right? You want to be known as a slut, and screw guys you aren't even dating, be my frigging guest."

Beth's gaze sank to the sidewalk. "Fine, Angel." She shook her head. "I knew you wouldn't understand."

I averted my eyes from the defeated expression on her face. "You know, Beth, maybe you've been looking up to the wrong person."

I took off toward school, away from Beth, away from not understanding. Why did it seem like my best friend and my mother felt it was okay to choose guys over me? I had all these strong feelings inside me, with nothing to do with them. When I hit the street corner it became clear. Crystal. I took a right instead of the direction of the school. Because I was good and ticked off and I knew exactly who deserved most of my grief.

Miguel "Badman" Badalin.

Miguel's garage door was open. Good, then I didn't have to bruise my knuckles pounding my frustrations on his front door. The guys were hanging out, eating junk food and watching television. A familiar music theme sounded from the screen.

I couldn't believe it, but the vandal posse was watching the program "COPS," of all shows. I would have laughed if I wasn't so pissed.

I power-walked up the driveway, but halted right before the raised door, not crossing the line inside. It made me feel better to not really be in his home when I told him what an absolute *jerk* he was.

"What's up, Angel," Rock called out in between munching on Doritos. I was too pumped up to answer back.

Miguel lounged on the couch. He had to know I was pissed. Why else would he look so self-satisfied?

I stuffed my hands in my sweatshirt's front pocket. "I want out."

Someone lowered the volume of the TV. The only noise was birds chirping from a nearby tree.

Miguel tilted his head back. "That right?"

I shifted. "Yeah."

He stood up slowly. "So you're just another toy."

"And you're just another backstabbing ass."

Disgust filled his face. "What the hell are you talkin' about?"

I scanned the stunned, eager faces of the crew. "Do you really want me to say it in front of everyone?"

"Go ahead. I don't give a fu—"

"Fine. You only asked me to be in the crew because of my friendship with Nathan. You got something against him from past drama, and you were just using me to get back at him."

He snorted. "Using you how? You're the one who wanted to learn graf. You're the one who wanted me to teach you."

Yeah, but he'd sought me out. He'd approached me. "So why'd you tell Nathan that we kissed after you and I were done? *Why'd you mess around with my best friend?*"

I saw Derek jerk his gaze to Miguel's back. Derek hadn't known. Maybe he really liked Beth . . .

"Eh," Miguel said, shrugging both shoulders. "You didn't want to put out, I found someone who would. And since you and Nathan were gettin' all close, I thought he should know what I *did* get from you."

"Whatever. This time I'm really done, Miguel. After the battle, I'm out of the crew."

He quickly strode toward me and I almost stepped back at the sudden flash of anger on his face. But I held still. He was trying to bluff me like usual. Scare me.

I was wrong. Suddenly his hands shot out. I flew backward. I hit the ground, my elbows stinging from the impact of concrete. Miguel loomed over me. The prick had pushed me.

He pushed me.

I curled my hands into fists, clenched my teeth. My heart was beating fast, my scalp tingling with perspiration. I shoved myself to my feet and launched myself at him. All I felt was hot, like steam pushing through my body.

Miguel raised his arms as if trying to block me. My right hand connected with the top of his head. His fist hit my shoulder. After that it all blurred with flying arms and pain. *Fast, fast. Hot, hot.* Then the guys were pulling us apart.

"Guys, chill out!"

"Bitch!"

"Asshole!"

Rock and Derek held Miguel back. Petey and Mateo secured my arms, but I was done fighting. My mouth was dry. I swallowed, trying to calm my breathing. My hands were shaking and I clenched them tight. "I'm cool," I told them. *"Let go."* They released me.

Miguel wasn't done. *"You* don't say you want out of the crew! Don't work that way, *chica. I* decide. And I've decided I'm tired of your mouth. Tired of your wack style. You don't hang with us no more. *You don't even know us."*

"This ain't cool, Miguel," Petey spoke up, then started squirming beside me when Miguel shot him a dirty look.

"So what?" Miguel asked. *"You* want out of the crew?"

"Naw," Petey answered, fingering one of his hair spikes. "I was just saying . . ."

Miguel jerked himself away from the guys, looked at me. If looks could inflict pain, I'd be back on the ground again in straight agony. "You're nothing. Get out of my face."

I brushed off my jeans. I was suddenly tired. Aches sprouted from my fall, shoulder pulsing. I just wanted to be gone. I could have let Miguel's words get me down, but I knew he wasn't worth it. He'd already put me through so much crap, it wasn't even funny. What grated most of all was that I had let him because I wanted to belong to a world of art I thought would accept me.

If being kicked out of the crew was the only way to get my life back on track, with my art and everything else, fine. Yeah, I could have used a hand with my graf style. There was still a lot for me to learn, but help wasn't an option anymore. Not from him. I had to compete in the battle or face a beat-down so I'd be there when the time came, and then Miguel wouldn't be part of my problems anymore.

Petey put a hand on my shoulder. "Damn, you okay?"

I just nodded and walked away with as much pride as I could hold together.

chapter fifteen

TOY
An Inexperienced Writer
Who Has a Wack Style
      –Angel's Piecebook Notes
        (No one wants a toy around.)

Stepping onto school grounds, my body might have been aching but my emotions were numb. I knew I needed to get my pack, grab my homework, but school was the furthest thing from my mind. Still, I went through the motions, walked down the hallway to my locker. I wasn't sure of the time. The school remained open for a couple hours after school for activities and stuff . . .

My hand froze on my locker combo.

The mural meeting, Rodriguez!

I turned on the balls of my feet and ran toward the courtyard. My stomach felt knotted and I didn't know what the hell I'd say to Nathan.

The committee was cleaning up when I made it to the courtyard. Nathan spotted me, then continued gathering supplies. I swallowed and made my way over to him.

"Nathan . . ."

"Just give me a minute."

I nodded and tried to help pick up some paint bottles.

"It's all right. I got it."

"Sure," I said, stuffing my hands in my pockets. I walked to a bench and leaned against it. I noticed a couple of the committee members look at me, then away.

Minutes later, Nathan strolled up to me. He wasn't smiling.

"This isn't the first meeting you've missed, Angel."

"I know." Was this the second? No way it was the third. "I'm sorry. There was this thing with Beth, and then—"

He glanced at me before staring somewhere behind me. "Miguel, right?" I knew he wasn't looking at anything specific, just not wanting to look at me.

And for a quick moment I wished for a mirror. I probably looked all messed up from the fight. I lifted a hand and pulled out my loose hair band. "It's not what you think," I said quietly.

"It never is. Look, Mr. Chun called me into his office after school. He says your GPA has slipped." He finally met my eyes. "I'm sorry, Angel. You're off the committee."

For some dumb reason, my throat seemed too thick to swallow. I looked away from him and nodded my head.

He cursed under his breath. "You know, I don't get it. I thought after lunch we were cool, then you ditch me and the committee for Miguel. I thought this project meant something to you."

"It did. It does."

"Yeah, I can tell." He shook his head. "Well, one good thing came out of this."

I met his eyes.

"Now you have all the time you want to hang with Miguel and create graffiti pieces, Grafangel."

He thought I wanted to spend time with Miguel rather than him. He headed the committee, it meant something to him, and in his eyes I'd turned my back on him. I knew I'd given up on putting any real effort into this mural once I found out my park wasn't involved in the community project, but I had vowed I would stay involved for Nathan's sake. And I had failed him, as if our friendship hadn't meant that much. As if the crew had meant more to me than to be with him. After today at his house, I had thought he'd understood it wasn't like that with Miguel. But he didn't believe me.

There was nothing more to say. I pushed off the bench and turned away.

"Angel," Nathan called but I couldn't look back.

Home. I just wanted to be home.

"Tell me, *m'ija*."

I sat next to Nana on the couch, her arms secured around me, my head resting on her soft shoulder. Her rose-scented powder filled my nose as tears streamed down my face. I'd always been a quiet crier. As if I was afraid of people knowing I was crying. As if I was afraid to show people I could be hurt or be sad. It hurt more to cry quietly. Tears didn't fall often from me, so when I did cry, it was like a spilled bucket of paint, pouring and pouring out, then the rest seeping out until every last drop was gone.

The bus ride home had been tough. It had given me plenty of time to think about how much my life sucked right now. How everything had gone wrong. I'd walked into my house with a big pressure in my chest and tightness in my throat. I had tried to avoid Nana's eyes, trying to get past her to the bathroom, but she kept talking to me, asking me how my day went and when she saw the strain on my face, she'd gotten this concerned expression and asked what was wrong.

And that had been the end of trying not to cry.

Now Nana stroked my hair after I let so much out. Told her about Nathan and Miguel, joining the crew, my fight with Beth, and how I'd been banned from the committee. The one thing I had wanted to be a part of in the first place. All through the confession, I continued to bawl like a baby.

Yeah, I held back about the bombing of the park. Maybe I was scared and embarrassed to have actually broken the law in such a big way. This wasn't a small piece of Laffy Taffy lifted from the liquor store without paying. This was cops looking for me, wanting me to be arrested and to face the consequences of the crime. Maybe I was worried Nana would look at me differently. Be disappointed. Not love me as much. Maybe it was all those things.

I was so upset, another hand running down my hair startled me. My mother had come home and I hadn't even heard the front door open.

"What is it, Angel?" she asked.

I turned to her and sniffed. *I need a tissue so bad.* I scrubbed my tears with the back of my hand. "I'm sorry. I didn't mean to come home so late that night. Or worry you and Nana." I blew out a breath. "I didn't mean to say anything bad. About you. The men you date."

She pulled me into her arms.

"Okay, my Angel, okay."

I felt the couch shift beside me. Nana was getting to her feet to give us time alone.

"I didn't steal the money," I said. "I make money at school, forging notes. It's a way to pay for my art stuff. I know we don't have the money to spend for my supplies."

I felt Mom's chest rise and fall. I pulled away.

"Your artwork really means that much to you," she murmured.

It wasn't really a question but I nodded. I looked down at my hands in my lap. "It's the only thing in my life I feel good doing. That I can lose myself in without even trying. I know it sounds ignorant but somehow it balances me. Art is a way to be my own person. To express myself. It's the only thing I have that is completely mine. It makes me feel . . ." I lifted a hand, looking for the right word.

"Special," Mom offered.

"Maybe." I sniffed. But yeah, wasn't that it? My art was such a big part of my life, it made me feel different, unique from other people at school. That's why I wanted to be so great at it. Because with the art crowd there was always someone better than me, who had a hell of lot more talent. Being with the crew, I thought I had a chance to shine above others but now on my own I might never get the chance.

"Everyone wants to feel special, Angel. Even me."

I looked at her. "Is that why, you know, you always date?"

She smiled and leaned against the back of the couch. "I like dating. Meeting new people is good for me. I want a distraction after a grueling day waiting tables when my makeup runs and my legs and feet are sore. Yeah, sometimes the right man manages to even make me feel special.

"You know, I don't set out in a relationship thinking it will fall apart. I know sometimes I don't have the best judgment when it comes to men, like José. What was I thinking there?" She shook her head, smiled. "But I do want to find the right man I can have a future with. Someone who might one day be a father to you."

I made a face at that, which only made her smile.

"I never know when that will happen, but I'm not going to sit at home and wait for it to happen. I know you don't understand. Maybe when you're older, you will." She sighed. "Look at us. We may not see eye to eye, but all I know is I want a better future for you than waiting tables at the local restaurant." She shook her head. "And I'm sorry, I don't think art will get you that better future."

"You don't know that," I whispered, although I wasn't all that convinced myself. It kind of hurt to hear her say it again even after we were finally talking things out, but maybe we weren't supposed to understand, maybe we were just supposed to accept each other the way we were.

"I know. And it's fine you're on this art committee if it makes you happy . . ." Something must have shown on my face. "What?"

"I've been kicked off."

"I'm sorry. I know how hard you had worked on your presentation."

I nodded. "That was before I knew our park wouldn't be added to the community art project."

"What do you mean?"

I told my mom about the murals and how North Caesar had been excluded.

She ran a hand back through her hair. "Angel, you'll learn

like I have, that people are going to overlook our neighborhood, or try to make us feel beneath them just because we live on a poorer side of town. You have to learn not to let it get you down."

"I guess. But I love that park."

She smiled. "I used to take you there when you were little and push you on the swings."

"Those are my best memories of us together," I whispered.

She met my eyes and I knew she understood. Something I'd been keeping even from myself. North Caesar was a part of me, a part of my childhood, a time that I could remember when there weren't any problems between us. When we laughed all the time, when there were no boyfriends standing between us. When she paid attention only to me.

I could see her pushing me on the swing. I would pump my legs as hard as I could, her laugh sounding behind me as she pushed me so high I thought I could touch the sky. More memories came of us sitting on the grass having a snack, tasting each other's ice cream. The days I would be so tired and I was still little enough for her to pick me up and carry me home as I rested my head against her shoulder . . .

Mom's eyes glistened and she blinked. "Some of my best memories, too."

My lips curved. The phone rang and I heard Nana answer it.

"Now tell me. What happened earlier? Did you have a fight with Beth?"

"It's a long story."

"Monica, phone," Nana called out from the kitchen.

"Tell whoever it is I'll call back," Mom said over her shoulder, then to me, "I have the time for a long story from my daughter."

And it was amazing . . . she did.

chapter **sixteen**

CREW
A Group of Writers Who Also
Tag the Crew Initials with Their Name
> —Angel's Piecebook Notes
> *(My crew was nowhere to be found.)*

all week I practiced my graffiti style, on paper and on a small plywood board I convinced my mom to let me set up in our overgrown backyard. I told her about graffiti style and a competition I needed to practice for, leaving out the breaking-the-law details about last Saturday. She was hesitant, but we had made a deal to be supportive of each other's interests and we were doing our best.

I could have just walked away from my commitment to the

battle, but always having to look over my shoulder for retaliation from the opposing crew was not my idea of fun. Besides, I had something to prove not only to Miguel, but to myself.

Somehow I managed to avoid everyone at school, hanging out with a girl in my English lit class a few times during lunch, other times painting in the art room with Mr. Chun's permission.

I'd hardly ever crossed paths with the crew anyway. Beth and I managed to go to our lockers at different times by carrying around most of our books for classes. Miguel and I didn't even look in each other's direction during art class. In fact, I hardly met Nathan's eyes, either, but come Friday, I guess he couldn't handle the silent treatment anymore.

"Did something happen with you and Miguel?" he asked me quietly before I could take my chair somewhere else and start on a new still life project. I'd been working in different parts of the class most of the week.

I hesitated, holding my hardboard, clipped with a thick watercolor sheet. I really didn't know where my relationship with Nathan stood. He'd tried to call me a couple times at home, but I never returned his messages. I figured he finally got the hint I didn't want to talk to him. I knew it wasn't his fault that I was off the committee, but for him to think I was seeing both him and Miguel or choosing Miguel over him wasn't okay with me. Made me think he didn't really know me all that well. Maybe it was the same for both of us.

"Guess you could say that," was all I said. I grabbed my stuff and chair and set up to work on the other side of the room.

When the bell rang, ending class, I slipped on my heavy pack and walked to Mr. Chun's desk. He was talking to another student and I waited a couple minutes as they finished.

He looked over at me and folded his hands on top of his desk. "Yes, Angel?"

I kicked my shoe on the floor and cleared my throat. "Well, I just wanted to say I'm sorry I messed up being on the committee."

"I'm sorry too, Angel. I was disappointed. You would have been a great asset to the project."

I nodded and started to turn away.

"Angel?"

"Yeah?"

"There'll be other projects, other contests. It's a waste if you don't try your best."

"I know. It's just . . ." I looked at his desk, then back to meet his eyes. "I'm not happy with my style of art. I don't feel it's strong enough."

"Strong enough for who?"

"Well, me, I guess."

He pushed up his glasses. "Then work harder, Angel. You have an individual talent and determination many students don't possess. Yes, your style is whimsical, but that's a strength, not a detriment. Use that to your advantage. If you keep at your work, you can make things happen for you."

I smiled. "Thanks." Maybe Mr. Chun had a point. Maybe I did have enough determination to get what I wanted in life. I knew I wanted a future in art . . . I just didn't know what kind yet.

Walking out of class with Mr. Chun's words ringing in my head, I spotted Beth walking toward me. Our eyes collided and she looked away.

I continued on to my locker, wishing we could go back to how we once were before I joined the crew. When I thought she was my best friend. When I didn't know she had looked up to me and I hadn't known I'd let her down.

I blew out a breath. Time to focus on the battle. I had thought I'd feel ready by the time the day arrived, different. But I was just the same Angel as three weeks ago.

And ready or not, it was time to battle.

"I'll be out in a minute!" The banging on the door stopped. I stared into Mark Billings's bathroom mirror.

It was almost as if a stranger looked back me. I'd just finished applying my mother's dark maroon lipstick, black eyeliner, and brown eye shadow. My hair was down and wavy with the help of hair gel. I reached for the hem of my hoodie, pulled it over my head, and shook out my hair.

I winced, pulling the long-sleeved shirt away from my breasts. It was a lost cause. The top I'd scrounged out of my closet fit like a second skin. It cut above my belly button, and with my low-hip army pants I'd be giving everybody a nice eyefull.

Since I was forced to be in this battle under false pretenses, I figured I'd dress the part, as well.

I'd actually arrived here with Miguel, which was a shocker, but he'd sent Petey up to me at school to say that he insisted on keeping up appearances as a crew. That he'd pick me up and take me to the battle tonight.

Yeah, one big, nice, happy crew. Now that was funny.

So I'd sought out the bathroom and pulled out the makeup I'd thrown in my pack. The guys probably thought I was so nervous I was making myself sick. Nervous, yeah. I rubbed my fluttering stomach. Sick, not yet. I took a last swig from a Red Bull and tossed the can in the wastebasket.

The pounding on the door started again and this time I grabbed my stuff and swung open the door. Some idiot fell forward. I moved back as he crumpled at my feet, moaning. I stepped over him and found Petey at the end of the hall waiting for me.

He glanced at me, looked away, and did a double take. His eyes were wide as he looked me up and down.

I tried not to smile. "We ready?"

He nodded, making his spikes move. "Yeah, they're waiting for you out back."

I took a breath. "Let's do this."

"Hey, good luck, Angel."

"Thanks, Petey."

We carved a path through partiers until we made it outside. Not many paid attention to me. After all, the real battle tonight was with Miguel and Maya—two top graf artists. I would just be a sideshow to them.

The moon was full with dark clouds passing over it, then revealing it again. The wind pushed good and hard through the air, but it wasn't as cold as I'd expected.

Twigs crunched under our feet as we walked down toward the plywood boards nailed against the wooden fences. I could see Miguel in the distance, leaning against his board, which was two feet away from mine. Smoke drifted around him. I nodded at Petey as we reached the crowd, and made my way through the watchers to my board.

When Miguel saw me, he stared. Took a long pull of his cigarette, then threw it down.

I didn't say anything to him, but unzipped my pack to start to line up my cans. I heard his steps as he walked toward me.

"You choose now to look fine," he said, his voice flat.

I shook my head. "You're such an ass, Miguel."

"I try," was all he said. "Don't fuck this up." With that thrilling advice he turned and walked away.

Lined up at my feet were three spray cans of each color I needed, except for black. I had five blacks. I felt pumped and ready. I rolled my shoulders, rotated my neck, and did a little hop. Dried leaves crunched under my feet. From my right,

Miguel looked at me kind of weird. What can I say, Red Bull gives you wings.

Across from us was another fence with two more pieces of plywood nailed up with the Maya guy and Braid Girl standing in front of it. A single light was in the middle of us, giving all the illumination we were going to get. Which amounted to the glow of a flashlight. Great.

The watchers slowly started to gather around us. I got a little antsy as more and more arrived to watch, but tried not to look at them, tried to ignore them.

The one aspect of piecing I hadn't gotten used to was not being able to sketch out my piece before I began. Sure, I sketched my piece on paper before, practiced over and over again on my small wooden board at home, but here I had to get it right. Here, I had to outline, then touch up when I could but couldn't afford mistakes during the battle. One wrong spray could throw off the entire design.

My gut did a little twist. *Mierda*, I was psyching myself out. *Not good, Rodriguez. Not good.*

Someone tapped me on the shoulder and I turned around.

Braid Girl. Veronica.

She lifted her chin toward me. "Be ready, *chica*. My style's gonna stomp you to the ground."

I rolled a shoulder, looking at her with disinterest. "Do what you can and we'll see."

She stared at me weird—as if expecting some sort of big,

bad comeback, but any big and bad I had going on was only on the outside.

"Yeah, everyone will see who's the *real* graf writer." She left with that big, bad response hanging in the air between us. Good for her.

I stared out into the crowd, my gaze moving over unfamiliar faces. One *chica* was talking with another, but she must have been flying high because she was bouncing around, her hands gesturing wildly. The guy standing a couple of heads to her right was picking his nose. Sick. More people talking, some laughing. Then my eyes collided with Nathan's and I froze.

In the dark, I saw him give a small smile. Beth stood next to him. What were they doing here? Was Nathan trying to show his support? But what about Beth? She had to be here for Miguel.

Or was she trying to hook up with Nathan now?

Why did they have to come? I turned back to face my blank board and saw nothing. No design, no color. How could the two people who I had royally messed up with be here? Why did Nathan have to show up and remind me what I had given up in order to be where I was now? And why did Beth have to come, when I wasn't even sure we could be best friends again?

Mark Billings walked between the two boards that separated the four us.

Hoots and hollers sounded from the watchers.

He raised his hands and nodded as if he was royalty. "Settle.

To the right we have West Coast Vandals, M&M man and B-Mac. To the left *Reyes del Norte*, Badman and GrafAngl. It's going to be a long two hours so everyone relax, chill, and have a good time. Don't distract the writers, fools. Let's get this party started."

Your wack style.

Whimsical, cartoon style.

Art's not going to get you anywhere.

You're nothing.

Cans rattled, spraying paint. My gut tightened even more. My palms were damp. I picked up a white can with a skinny cap attached and noticed my hand shaking.

Damn.

"Move it, Angel," Miguel called out to me. "What's your problem?"

"Nothing," I muttered. But yeah, I knew what was the matter. If I didn't pull this piece off, I'd be known as a "toy" in front of these people, a good portion of them graf writers. Word would likely spread from graffiti crew to crew. People at NHH would likely find out and whisper behind my back.

There's the chica *who tried to be a graffiti artist and failed. She couldn't even hack it with basic art, either. Got kicked off the mural committee. What a poser.*

Part of the reason for joining the crew was to find my place in the art world. If I didn't prove myself here, I didn't think my style would fit anywhere.

No direction. No friends.

Just me with my messed-up style that would feel hollow and flat.

Miguel walked up to me. "Damn, why don't you just forfeit now. You're givin' the crew a bad rep."

My hand squeezed the can. "Get off my back, Jack."

"Once a toy, always a toy," he whispered in my ear.

I shoved him away and he stepped back, an irritating half smile curving his mouth. The one I'd thought was cute when I'd first met him.

"We'll see who's the toy, Badman." I pressed my finger on the nozzle and started outlining my piece.

"Way to go, Angel!" I glanced over at Beth. She was cheering me on. Somehow, even after all that had happened, her voice felt natural and comforting. After all, hadn't she always been my number one cheerleader?

"Kick ass, Angel." Definitely Nathan's voice.

And then everything else was blocked out, pushed out of my mind. My piece finally popped into my head. I could see it so clear, so bright.

My hand was moving, moving, moving.

My lines smooth and going just where I wanted.

I could do this. I could create my piece. Because I just realized one important fact . . .

I'd finally mastered the spray can.

Yeah, I still needed to push the limits with my graf style in order to stand out among other writers, but I was at ease with my medium. Knowing how to wield a can meant I could work my style on my own. I didn't need Miguel or anyone to help further my skill. It would come in time with practice. I didn't have to be the best graf writer out there. The world wouldn't end if I didn't win this competition. Maybe pleasing myself was good enough.

Since losing the mural contest, I'd felt alone. Unskilled. Basically felt I sucked. But there was one thing I could be proud of—I'd worked my ass off learning graf and improving my style. My hard work had paid off. I could succeed in any type of art I set my mind to.

The only person who had to respect my art was me.

Time flew by as I painted, losing myself inside the piece. The outline of the girl was the most difficult, but I'd been drawing and painting this piece for the past week and it was all about how close you painted and how quickly you moved your hand across the wood. Going over the outline the last time, hoping my lines didn't become too harsh and jerky, which could be a possibility since my right wrist and hand were starting to ache.

"Five minutes!" Billings called out.

I still had a few touch-ups so I flexed my hand and wiggled my stiff fingers. Wasn't used to going for so long.

With white, then black, I added highlights and shading in various spots of the girl I'd created. Before I knew it, the watchers were counting down . . .

". . . six . . . five . . . four . . ."

I dropped my can, there was no more to be done.

"... three ... two ... one ..."

"Times up!"

Taking a breath, I rotated my stiff neck. I hadn't looked at my competition. Didn't want to. Not yet.

I stared at my design, my piece. It was good. Damn good. "GRAFANGL" was written in rounded white letters, outlined in black. The letters were, yeah, whimsical, cartoony, but that was me. That was my strength and I finally embraced it. A teenage angel with long dark hair, wearing a hoodie, leaned against the name. Her arms crossed, a spray can in her hand. Small white wings attached to the back of her sweatshirt.

Crossing my arms, I leaned back against the fence next to my design. Fatigue weighed on my body, but I stood there for the next ten minutes while Mark Billings and a couple of his sidekicks took the time to check out each piece.

Braids's piece was some weird-ass drawing of her tag: B-Mac, with twisted arrows that zigzagged in different directions. I thought her shadowing was a bit off, but it could have been just part of her style. She didn't have any real character. It seemed she put all her effort into making those arrows clean.

Between Miguel and Maya, I actually couldn't tell who would win. They were so skilled. Both of their pieces were of their tags but Miguel had a city behind his tag and a masked graf writer standing atop a building. Excellent.

Maya had two characters back to back over his tag, the colors brilliant and fading into one another so smoothly.

What would Billings base his decision on? I had no idea. Almost didn't matter. I felt so good about my work, I could have walked away right then without knowing—without caring—who came out the winner. Because in my own mind, I had won. But I didn't want to piss off any of my fellow writers. It could be seen as a sign of disrespect.

"Now, these are some sick-ass pieces, dawgs. I am impressed!" The watchers laughed and cheered. "But I must choose the winners of this tight battle." He ran a hand down his goatee. "And the winner between Badman and M&M man is . . . BADMAN."

Hoots and hollers erupted from the watchers.

I glanced over at Miguel. He raised his arms, nodding his head as if he had no doubt. Maybe he didn't. The guy had a serious case of egomania.

"Winner between Grafangl and B-Mac is . . . GRAFANGL."

More cheers. The crew appeared by my side, patting my back, ruffling my hair.

I'd won. I'd won all on my own.

The music shut off and I spotted kids running from the main house.

"What the hell?" someone said beside me.

"Raid!!"

"This is the police," a voice shouted through some kind of megaphone. "Stop running. Everyone get down on the ground with your hands on your heads."

"Shit," I hissed, looking toward the crew, but they were all gone. Scattered in the dark. I grabbed my unzipped pack and ran. Cans fell out. But I didn't know whether to leave them or try to gather them because of fingerprints. Damn, I watched too many cop shows.

My eyes jerked around as I ran.

No sign of Beth.

No Nathan.

Could have sworn I heard Nathan call my name. Not sure. Numerous flashlights were running across the grounds like some psychedelic freak show. I couldn't tell who was who, where any of the crew was.

Run to Miguel's ride.

But I knew that was a lost cause. He'd be gone, out for saving his own ass.

I started to run in the direction of the trees. It was freaking nuts, I knew. What could be in all those black trees? Wild animals? Homeless transients?

Freaking nuts.

Run!

I ran, my heart pumping wildly in my chest. My mouth, dry as dust.

"Stop! Police!" shouted from behind me.

My stomach felt like it dropped under my feet and I'd just stomped all over it.

Should I stop? Keep running?

Something *huge* rammed into my back. I lost my grip on

my pack. My whole body smashed into the hard ground. Rocks bit into my chest, my hands. My face burned against dry grass and twigs.

Damn, damn—ow!

"Dumb, kid. You. Shouldn't have . . . run," some guy heaved above me. He weighed a freaking ton. He coughed, nearly hacking up a lung. He pulled my hands behind my back, put something around my wrist that bit into my skin like hard plastic. He tugged, and the plastic tightened.

"Get off of me," I pushed out through gritted teeth.

He finally did, but with a hand on my wrists and one on my shoulder, he pulled me to my feet.

I spit out dirt and small pieces of dried grass.

Hair was hanging from my cheek, and I couldn't get it off because it was stuck to my sweat.

Some kids were still running around, cops yelling after them.

The cop led me up toward the house where a bunch of other people were sitting down in a line, hands behind their backs. It was tough to make out who was who, but I was pretty sure the crew had gotten away. The cop shoved me to the ground next to some kid who kept rocking side-to-side and mumbling, "Gonna get sick. Gonna get sick."

An officer placed a megaphone to his mouth and said, "You are all under arrest for public disturbance and will be questioned in connection to a recent vandalism crime. Each of you will be taken down to the station and your personal information taken, fingerprinted, and allowed a call home. If you're under age, your guardian will be contacted."

There were groans and curses for a response.

"Yeah, too bad. Listen up. You have the right to remain silent . . ."

"Gonna get sick. Gonna—"

The kid next to me puked all over his lap. A sour odor assaulted my nostrils. I turned my face away.

Yeah, I felt like puking, too. Because my piece was on that board down the hill created in front of a hundred witnesses.

The same tag that hit the newspapers as being wanted by police.

My knees bounced as I sat beside my mother in a small room inside the Homestead police station. A Detective Lorenzo with a noticeable overbite and five o'clock shadow sat on the other side of the table.

I looked down at the fingerprints on the table, visible under the glare of the light, and picked at the dry skin on my lips. I pulled too hard and my lip stung. Licking my lips, I tasted blood.

"Angel, we have almost a dozen witnesses who say they saw you paint the name GrafAngl at the party. We know you're involved in the vandalism at East Mason Park on October 5th. It's just a matter of you admitting to it on this piece of paper here." He shoved forward a yellow pad with a pencil on top. "And naming who was with you."

My mother cleared her throat. "Someone else could have painted the same name at the park."

"Mrs. Rodriguez—"

"Ms."

He paused. "Ms. Rodriguez, I've been following graffiti vandals for a long time. It's rare to see a copy done with such skill."

I lifted my eyebrows. He thought my piece was good? Okay, that probably wasn't that important right about now.

"Should you fail to inform us of the other vandals, you'll likely face time in juvenile detention. Is that what you want, Angel? To do time? To have a criminal record?"

I shook my head. I knew for certain now the crew had gotten away. They didn't have Miguel's name or his connection to "Badman." I guessed because I'd been caught, the others who had been caught as well had fingered me for my battle piece on the board, leaving out the names of the writers who'd gotten away.

"Give me names, Angel. Who else was with you the night of October 5th."

I folded my hands in my lap and stared down at the paint on my fingers.

Black, red, white, a smear of purple.

These last few weeks with the crew had taught me a lot of things, and one of them was not to backstab your friends. I couldn't give up the crew. I couldn't even give up Miguel even though he likely would have spit out my name the instant he was asked. To me, narcing on your crew didn't seem right. And yeah, I really had no allegiance to them since I'd been kicked out by Miguel or walked away on my own. If any of the crew wanted to turn themselves in, they could. I wasn't going to do that for them.

I could have tried to lay blame on someone else for being arrested, but I was the one who wanted to be a graf writer. I was the one who crossed lines, who went so far that I didn't think about all the repercussions of my actions. I had stepped further and further into an underground world of danger, art, and freedom, not caring that I was pushing myself further away from my best friend, the guy I truly cared for, even my mom. I'd made my choices all on my own. I couldn't blame anyone but myself. If nothing else, it was time to own up to my actions. To not just be respected as an artist, but respected as a good person.

"I did it alone. I bombed the park."

"Angel," my mother whispered.

I didn't look at her. I wasn't sure if she meant, "Angel, stop" or "Angel, how *could* you?"

"Who was with you?"

I swallowed. "No one."

The detective sighed. "You want to go to juvey, is that it?"

"No, what I want is to go home."

"You just happened to tag all those different names in different variations of expertise?"

I looked down at my hands, ignoring his question. "Did

you know . . . the parks in the richer part of town get more money to upgrade their equipment than the parks in the older neighborhoods? That my neighborhood gets older and run-down, and nobody does anything about it?"

He cleared his throat. "Vandalism is still against the law, Angel, and not the way to make a statement in the community. And no way to make a positive difference."

I shut my eyes. I wish I could say I did it to make a statement about social classes in our town. But I'd been selfish. I'd felt free piecing at the park, even though I'd known it was wrong.

Now I had to pay the consequences.

"I know," I told the detective. "But I did it all by myself."

chapter **seventeen**

FRESH
Cool and Good
—Angel's Piecebook Notes
(Starting new again.)

I stuffed my pack in my locker during lunch, slamming the door shut.

Selena Macgregor with her signature pastel pink lipstick stood beside me. "I got five bucks."

I shook my head, even though I was tempted to take her money for a forged note. "Shop's closed for good."

"What? You getting a real job now?"

"As a matter of fact." I'd filled out applications all week.

"Well, shit."

I smirked. "You could always stop ditching."

"If I wanted advice from a criminal, I would have asked." She turned on her heel and walked away.

Yeah, word had spread in the two weeks since my arrest. I now had a rep as a vandal among the faculty of NHH, maybe even to some of the kids who didn't know a paintbrush from a charcoal pencil. Turned out law enforcement had buckled down in order to stop the recent spike in town graffiti vandalism and as retaliation for the huge bombing we did at the skate park. The raid at Mark Billings's house was just what the mayor had reportedly ordered.

Lucky me, my judge didn't try to make too much of an example of me. I managed to skip time in a juvenile detention center by agreeing to two years of community service to help clean up city parks. It may not be painting murals, but hey, it's something I wanted to do in the first place and a heck of a lot better than facing juvey time.

"Such a bitch," I murmured at Selena's retreating back.

"Tell me about it."

My stomach tightened as I turned to see Beth behind me. She wore faded jeans, a white tee, and blue zip-up hoodie. Her blonde hair was in a ponytail and a small smile played on her lips.

"Hey," I said. "How's it going?"

"Good. You?"

I shrugged. "All right."

I never found out who Beth was at the battle to support,

me or Miguel. Really, it didn't matter anymore. I'd gotten over Miguel. I'd gotten over feeling betrayed by Beth. Time does that, lets you get over things.

"Look, I wanted to tell you some stuff," she said as she looked at the scuffed floor in front of me, then up to meet my eyes. "Can we talk?"

It was lunch and I had been about to meet a couple of girls I'd hung out with in junior high. Could I talk with Beth? Did I want to? Yeah, I did. I missed hanging out with her.

"Sure." We went to the food court and bought our usual—turkey Subway sandwiches, ranch Doritos, and two cans of cola—and went to sit on the grassy area behind the bleachers on the field. Like old times, but not really. Times had changed.

Beth held the sandwich in front of her and sighed. "I didn't sleep with Miguel because of you."

I didn't say anything for a minute, but the chunk of guilt in my chest finally loosened. "Why did you?"

"It's true that when you joined the crew I started to feel like I was losing my best friend. Suddenly there was this group of guys it seemed you wanted to be with more than me." She finally took a bite of her sub, chewed, then continued. "Guys you could feel a connection with through art, something I had no talent at whatsoever. I felt weird about it. Didn't know how to deal. Suddenly Miguel starts showing interest in *me*. I guess because he's so hot there was no way I was passing him up. I mean I've gone out with some cute guys but Miguel is way up there, you know?"

I nodded because yeah, I agreed. But I'd come to realize looks don't mean as much when you're a total ignorant jerk.

"That night I went with him and Rock, we were just hanging out in the garage when Miguel asked me into his house to check out some of his work. My heart was beating really fast. I knew he was pissed at you for brushing him off. Figured he might want to even the score, but I wasn't sure how until he started touching me. Before I knew it we were kissing. I was so flattered, so jazzed he wanted me. I wasn't exactly his type with my big hips and boobs, you know? So maybe I gave him hints I was willing to go further if he wanted. I knew it would be a one-time thing, why not get somebody I really wanted?

"Maybe . . . I thought he might even want to see me again because I slept with him. Maybe I thought in some weird out-of-this-world way that we could end up dating."

She looked down at her sandwich. "Now that Miguel got what he wanted, he won't talk to me. He won't even look in my direction when I see him at school. Then it all hit me, how I totally betrayed your trust doing all of this behind your back. I never wanted to hurt you. I just wanted something really bad and I took it."

Yeah, I couldn't blame her for setting her sights on something, then taking it when she had the chance. Wasn't that what I'd done with graffiti? I'd set my sights on learning it and gone for it without thinking of the repercussions.

"It's true I look up to you. You're so confident with your-self, like you don't care who pays attention to you. I wanted to be like that. I wish I could."

I patted her shoulder. "I'm sorry, Beth."

That was all I could say right now. Because this one "sorry" covered so many things . . .

That I'd let the crew and Miguel come between us, that we'd fought in the first place, that even though it wasn't my fault, I was still sorry Miguel had sex with her and then dumped her.

"Hey, I'm a big girl. I can roll with the punches."

"I wish I could have really been that person to look up to for you. But just like anybody, I've had my own insecurities. My own doubts to deal with. I'm slowly trying to work them out. The way you have to do, too," I said.

"It's probably time for a change with me and guys. Slow-ing down a bit."

"If that's what you want, it sounds like a plan."

I smiled and so did she. And just like that, everything was okay. We both knew we'd start hanging out again. But maybe we both understood it wouldn't be the same as before. It would be a little different this time. We just had to wait and find out how.

As I was prepping a paint pallet, a long tanned hand holding a piece of paper slid into my field of vision. I smelled his mild cologne and knew it was Nathan. Even though I hadn't talked much to him these last few weeks, my stomach fluttered just being close to him again.

A list of locations in Homestead were typed in a column on the paper. Some were parks, an old restaurant, the city post office, and old town stores that had been built over forty years ago.

Near the bottom one park was highlighted: North Caesar Park.

Somehow Nathan had gotten my neighborhood park added to the city's mural program.

I turned around. "How?"

"I wrote a report on some of the neglected parks in town. Got some signatures. It took a couple of weeks but I just got word it was one of the parks added. Even if our school doesn't win the contest, it will at least have a town mural painted by the winners."

I felt myself smiling. "I can't believe you did this." I can't believe I hadn't thought it could be this simple. I'd let my neighborhood cloud my judgment, thinking because of where I lived that I couldn't make a difference.

"Believe it."

"I don't know what to say."

" 'Thanks' might work."

"Thanks, Nathan. This is cool. Really cool."

He met my eyes and smiled. "You're welcome. It's my way of also saying sorry."

"For what?"

He rubbed the back of his neck. "That day I let you go from the committee . . . I could have handled it better. Before the mural meeting I had a fight with my dad on my cell, about the committee, of course. I took my problems out on you. That wasn't cool. It's not even an excuse."

"Hey, it was my fault I screwed up my chances. Don't worry about it."

He shook his head. "That's not all the way true. I figured you were choosing Miguel over me. I didn't stand back enough to realize you wouldn't do that. By the time I thought it out, you wouldn't return my calls. Wouldn't even look in my direction during class."

He continued to look at me, studying my face. He said softly, "I'm sorry, Angel. I'd like for us to talk again."

My cheeks warmed and I cleared my throat. "Sure."

chapter **eighteen**

WRITER
A Practitioner of Graf Art
—Angel's Piecebook Notes
(Me.)

It took a little maneuvering. Getting to know my community service supervisor a little better, performing my work every other day after school for two hours and five hours on Saturday. But in the end it worked out and I managed to have us hit North Caesar Park for cleanup the same day they began the community mural.

Nathan and the rest of the mural committee were there, of course, since they'd won the competition. Mr. Chun was there, too. Maybe I was picking up trash while they started painting the base coat for the mural, but I was there. It was good enough.

I just hadn't expected someone else to show up.

"Eh, Angel, what's up?"

I was sitting under a tree, taking a fifteen-minute break. I twisted the cap on my water bottle and set it down beside me. "Nothing much, Miguel."

I didn't get up.

Why should I make it easy for him? Truthfully, I didn't have any more anger for Miguel. I just accepted that he was a jerk, who only cared about himself, and that I never had to be friends with him again and really didn't want to.

And here he was. Not alone. Petey had wandered over to the mural committee to check out the progress. He waved to me. I waved back.

I only had a few more minutes before I had to get back to work. So I skipped the pleasantries. "What do you want?"

"Something's been bugging me for a while."

I finally glanced up at him. He looked the same other than the fact that he wasn't wearing his usual smirk. Baggy black jeans, this time a gray T-shirt, and he fingered his wallet chain hanging from his pocket.

I lifted my eyebrows in question.

"Why didn't you give us up?"

Obviously he was talking about my not telling the police that he and the crew had been with me at our bombing of

East Mason Park. I knew why I hadn't, but did I really need Miguel to know?

Maybe I did. Because there was something I wanted to know myself.

"The code," I said.

He nodded in understanding.

"I have a question for you. Did you really start hanging out with me because of Nathan?"

He wiped a hand over his mouth as if trying to hide a grin. He wasn't very successful.

"Ain't gonna lie. Yeah. But I found something out in the process."

"What's that?"

"That maybe you turned out to be an all right graf artist, anyway. Take it easy, Angel." He turned and walked away.

I couldn't stop my smile. What I would have given to have heard him say that weeks ago. Now I was in a place where I no longer needed his affirmation. It wasn't about whether I was good or bad, or who was better or worse. It was about doing something with my art, making something of my talent, and most of all accepting my own style. Accepting myself.

I sat there another moment, watching Nathan instruct the committee on what to do next. He turned and smiled at me. I smiled back. Nathan and I had had a long talk and we were giving dating a try again. I was doing my best not to worry about our street addresses. Nathan didn't care how differently we lived. He just wanted to get to know me better.

We're both still pursuing our art.

Just different styles.

I'm set on a new personal goal, to do my best to prove to my community that graffiti art isn't just about illegal vandalism. It is about artistic freedom that can be expressed through public murals and even graffiti clubs. I'd done my research on bigger cities that had accomplished these things, gradually collecting ideas along with my community service supervisor, Mr. Garcia. He thought I was nuts, but he was playing along.

I knew I had my work cut out for me, especially after the bombing of the park, but my experiences had taught me a lesson and given me a reason to change. I wanted to open other people's eyes the way my own eyes had been opened. There was no way I was giving up practicing graf.

After all, I was no longer just a graffiti girl.

I'm a real graffiti writer.

Your attitude. Your style.
MTV Books:
Totally your type.

Cruel Summer

First in the *Fast Girls, Hot Boys* series!

Kylie Adams

Life is a popularity contest...and someone is about to lose. In sexy Miami Beach, five friends are wrapping up high school—but one of them won't make it to graduation alive....

The Pursuit of Happiness

Tara Altebrando

Declare your independence....After her mother dies and her boyfriend cheats on her, Betsy picks up the pieces of her devastated life and finds remarkable strength and unexpected passion.

Life as a Poser

First in the *310* series!

Beth Killian

Sometimes you have to fake it to make it....Eva spends an intoxicating summer in glamorous Hollywood with her famous talent agent aunt in this witty, pop culture-savvy novel, first in a new series.

Plan B

Jenny O'Connell

Plan A didn't know about him....When her movie-star half brother—a total teen heartthrob—comes to town, one very practical girl's plans for graduation and beyond are blown out of the water.

 BOOKS

Available wherever books are sold.

Published by Pocket Books
A Division of Simon & Schuster
A CBS Company

www.simonsays.com/mtvbooks

14330

Printed in the United States
By Bookmasters